"Where

Paul demanded, thrusting the tabloid under her nose. Glitzy photographs of him covered the front page. His stage name dotted sensational headlines.

"I—in St. Johnsbury," Pam stammered.

He dropped the paper on the desk and muttered a couple of expletives. "I guess my disguise has been pretty sorry, hasn't it?" he asked bitterly. And with a glance at the tabloid, he added, "You recognized me in those pictures, right?"

"Yes."

"But this doesn't come as a surprise, does it?" There was anger in his voice.

"What makes you say that?"

"Don't hedge, Pam. I'm right, am I not? This *doesn't* come as news to you. How long have you known?"

"How long? Well, I . . ."

"Come off it, Pam!" he commanded. "You knew who I was the minute you first saw me, didn't you?"

She nodded slowly. "Yes."

"Why didn't you say so?"

She swallowed. "It seemed obvious that you wanted to be . . . incognito."

Dear Reader,

At Silhouette Romance we're starting the New Year off right! This month we're proud to present *Donavan,* the ninth wonderful book in Diana Palmer's enormously popular LONG, TALL TEXANS series. *The Taming of the Teen* is a delightful sequel to Marie Ferrarella's *Man Trouble*—and Marie promises that Angelo's story is coming soon. Maggi Charles returns with the tantalizing *Keep It Private* and Jody McCrae makes her debut with the charming *Lake of Dreams.* Pepper Adams's *That Old Black Magic* casts a spell of love in the Louisiana bayou—but watch out for Crevi the crocodile!

Of course, no lineup in 1992 would be complete without our special WRITTEN IN THE STARS selection. This month we're featuring the courtly Capricorn man in Joan Smith's *For Richer, for Poorer.*

Throughout the year we'll be publishing stories of love by all of your favorite Silhouette Romance authors—Diana Palmer, Brittany Young, Annette Broadrick, Suzanne Carey and many, many more. The Silhouette Romance authors and editors love to hear from readers, and we'd love to hear from *you!*

Happy New Year... and happy reading!

Valerie Susan Hayward
Senior Editor

MAGGI CHARLES

Keep It
Private

Silhouette Romance

Published by Silhouette Books New York

America's Publisher of Contemporary Romance

With love, to Liz Argo...
a great TV pro and an even greater person

SILHOUETTE BOOKS
300 E. 42nd St., New York, N.Y. 10017

KEEP IT PRIVATE

ISBN: 0-373-08840-X

First Silhouette Books printing January 1992

All the characters in this book have no existence
outside the imagination of the author and have
no relation whatsoever to anyone bearing the same
name or names. They are not even distantly
inspired by any individual known or unknown
to the author, and all incidents are pure invention.

®: Trademark used under license and
registered in the United States Patent and
Trademark Office and in other countries.

Printed in the U.S.A.

MAGGI CHARLES

wrote her first novel when she was eight and sold her first short story when she was fifteen. Fiction has been her true love ever since. She has written forty-plus romance and mystery novels and many short stories. The former newspaper reporter has also published dozens of articles, many having to do with her favorite avocations, which include travel, music, antiques and gourmet cooking. Maggi was born and raised in New York City. Now, she and her writer husband live in a sprawling old house on Cape Cod. They have two sons and three grandchildren.

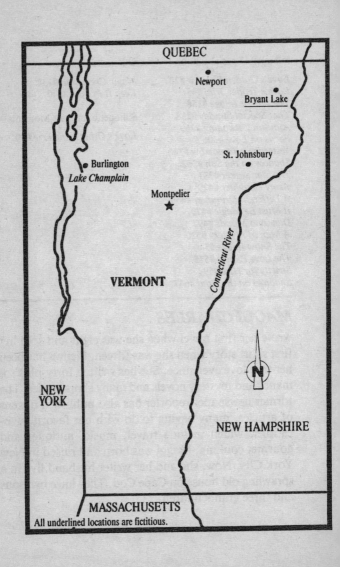

QUEBEC

Newport

Bryant Lake

Burlington
Lake Champlain

St. Johnsbury

Montpelier ★

Connecticut River

VERMONT

NEW
YORK

NEW HAMPSHIRE

MASSACHUSETTS

All underlined locations are fictitious.

Chapter One

The September sun had plenty of summer heat left over, even in northern Vermont. The late-morning rays blazed down on Pam as she pulled her big old convertible into the driveway beside Cullum's General Store and parked behind Chris Cullum's bright red Isuzu Trooper.

She climbed out of the car, pushed a tangle of damp, blond curls back from her forehead, and wished her yellow cotton shirt didn't feel as though it had been glued to her skin.

The store's shady interior was pleasantly cool, and it took a minute for Pam's eyes to adjust to the relative dimness. Then, as she glanced toward the man standing at the counter and talking to Bert Cullum, she froze. There, only a few feet away, was the one person in the world she'd hoped she'd never run into again.

He was wearing black-rimmed glasses, baggy chinos and a wrinkled blue work shirt. His dark hair was shaggy, and he could have done with a shave. But Pam would have known him anywhere.

Last time they'd met, she'd come off like an idiot.

Pam flinched . . . and started to backtrack. Immediately, a floorboard creaked.

Bert looked up and bellowed a hearty, "Hi there, Pam."

"Hi," Pam responded weakly.

Quickly she headed for the table against the far wall where Bert displayed locally baked breads, rolls, cakes and cookies. She picked up a bag filled with chocolate-chip cookies—something she'd not intended to indulge in—then turned toward the shelves stocked with canned fruits and vegetables, so that her back was to the counter.

Behind her, she heard that mellow, unforgettable voice say, "I think that's it. No, wait a minute. I'll take two cans of corned-beef hash."

A couple of seconds passed. Then Bert asked, "Sure that's everything?"

"For now, yes."

Pam heard the cash register clang—Bert Cullum had no use for modern computerized systems—and Bert announced, "That'll be forty-seven dollars and fifty-three cents, Mr. Martin."

Martin?

Pam frowned. Martin was *her* name—and she knew damned well it wasn't his!

There was a pause during which money evidently changed hands. Then Bert said, "I'll help carry your groceries out to your car."

"Thanks, but I can manage," replied the mellifluous voice that had stirred the hearts of most of the women in America at one time or another. "Go ahead and take care of your other customer."

Pam heard the screened front door snap shut. Only then did she turn, just as Bert called, "Need any help, Pam?"

She'd stopped in for a quart of milk and a six-pack of diet tonic. Now she'd accumulated the cookies, plus a can of peaches. She took her merchandise over to the scarred wooden counter and set the things down.

"You might dig one of your kosher dills out of the barrel, Bert," she suggested; then noticed the two full bags of groceries still on the counter. Obviously, the man masquerading under the name "Martin" would be returning any second.

Pam glanced around just in time to see him loom in the doorway. She said hastily, "I need a jar of applesauce, too," and retreated to the rear of the store.

For the next minute or so Pam fiddled around as if selecting applesauce were a life-and-death matter. Only when she heard *that* voice say, "Take it easy, Bert," and the door close, did she edge back toward the counter.

Bert was putting a fat dill pickle into a plastic bag. "Something else, Pam?" he asked cheerfully.

"No, thanks."

She took a ten-dollar bill out of her handbag before she realized she hadn't gotten what she'd come here for in the first place.

"Wait a sec," she grumbled, and made for the refrigerator. "I forgot I need milk and soda."

As she selected a carton of milk, Pam drew a deep, steadying breath. She needed to get control of herself before she went back to the counter, because she planned to ask Bert a few questions. As a starter, she'd inquire casually, "Who's Mr. Martin?" Then, when Bert answered, she could take it from there.

Was it possible that Bert Cullum didn't know his customer was Jason St. Clair, star of *When Tomorrow Comes,* the most popular daytime soap on TV?

Till two years ago, Pam had never seen a daytime drama. But when a bad case of flu kept her home for nearly three weeks, she'd turned on the television as an antidote to boredom. She'd never expected she could become interested in a soap, let alone hooked on one. Then, like millions of other female viewers, she'd quickly become mesmerized not so much by the story line of *When Tomorrow Comes,* as by Jason St. Clair, starring as Griffith McQueen, M.D.

St. Clair was traditionally tall, dark and handsome...but so much more than that. He was caring and compassionate, humorous and irresistible. There wasn't an ounce of meanness in his whole, gorgeous six-foot-two body. He was the proverbial knight in shining armor come to life in a modern world—strong, fearless, uncompromising . . . and devastatingly sexy.

Pam had succumbed to an instantaneous crush on him, and thoroughly enjoyed every minute of it.

Once she'd gone back to work, *When Tomorrow Comes* had, of necessity, lost out as part of her daily life. But from time to time she'd found herself picking up magazines that detailed the lives of TV stars.

For months, she'd continued to scoop up all the information she could unearth about Jason St. Clair. He was a native of Nebraska, who'd been "discovered" bartending at a trendy night spot in Omaha by a New York agent who saw potential in his striking good looks. He'd come East at the agent's urging, done TV commercials for a while, then played minor parts in several other soaps before heading straight for stardom as Griffith McQueen, M.D.

Off camera, he was an accomplished skier, and skilled enough at tennis to shine at celebrity benefit tournaments. When the show was in production, he lived in a penthouse condo in Manhattan overlooking the East River. Other times, he retreated to his private oasis in Antigua, or to his ski "chalet" near Aspen, Colorado.

Reportedly, he and Angela Santoro, his costar on *When Tomorrow Comes,* were having a torrid love affair. The gossip columnists indicated wedding bells in the offing—then warned that St. Clair would be a very hard man to catch, even for Angela Santoro. His oft-quoted stand on relationships with the opposite sex was: "Confirmed Bachelor."

Pam had gobbled up the juice on Jason St. Clair like a love-struck teenager, all the while passionately envious of Angela Santoro. She'd fantasized time and again about what it would be like to meet Jason St. Clair face-to-face, to spend even five minutes alone with him, maybe during a candlelit dinner....

Then the impossible had happened. She'd met Jason St. Clair in person, close up, one on one...for the most awkward half hour of her life.

Now Pam shrank from the memory and shuddered—and heard that voice she'd never forget, coolly say, "Miss, I think you're blocking my car."

Pam was so startled that she nearly dropped the carton of milk. Jason St. Clair instinctively reached out in an effort to divert possible disaster. Their hands brushed. But instead of soaring butterflies lighting up her inner world, Pam felt a cold chill sweep through her.

Any second now, he'd recognize her.

When nothing happened, she glanced up. The glasses he was wearing were slightly tinted, so they obscured his silvery-gray eyes. Nevertheless, she was aware that those eyes were sweeping her face. And though he spoke politely, he couldn't hide his impatience as he said, "I assume that convertible is yours?"

He didn't recognize her.

Pam didn't know whether to be relieved or affronted.

"It's mine, yes," she admitted.

"And the Isuzu's mine," he stated.

"I thought that was Chris Cullum's car." Pam turned toward the checkout counter, expecting Bert to verify the fact that the red Trooper belonged to his son. But another customer had come in the store and Bert was busy, heedless of what was going on.

"For your information," Jason St. Clair said shortly, "Chris Cullum has gone back to college, and I bought his car before he left. Now, would you kindly move *your* car so I can be on my way?"

Pam nodded, set the carton of milk aside and started for the door, painfully aware that the star of *When Tomorrow Comes* was right on her heels. Outside in the sun, she slipped behind the wheel of the big old car, trying to not so much as glance in his direction. But when she turned the key in the ignition and depressed the accelerator, not much happened. The engine growled once or twice, made a clicking noise, then growled again.

Pam groaned. She'd bought the car secondhand in Boston for the sole purpose of having transportation while at Bryant Lake. She had become increasingly sure she'd purchased a lemon and was planning on having it repaired at Hank Gibson's garage.

She'd only been back in Bryant Lake for two days, and this was her first visit in over four years. The last time she'd been at the lakeside cottage a couple of miles out of town, her father had been with her. They'd fished in the early mornings, hiked through the woods in the afternoons. Evenings, they'd watched the sun slide behind the mountains to the west, the afterglow spreading glory across the sky.

God, she still missed him so much....

Pam became aware of the tall figure standing beside her car door, and depressed the accelerator again. The engine coughed, choked, groaned, clicked...but still didn't catch.

She tried again, this time pumping the accelerator pedal furiously. The engine shrieked in protest. Already tense and frustrated, it didn't help to hear Jason St. Clair say frostily, "You're going to destroy the starter if you keep that up.... Hell, you've already flooded the engine!"

Pam shook her head. "I think it's more than that."

"What do you mean, you think it's more than that?"

"I may need a new battery. I don't know."

Pam pushed the car door open so abruptly that Jason St. Clair had to step aside fast or risk being hit. "I'll go over to the gas station and get Hank Gibson," she muttered.

The tall heartthrob actor actually blocked her way. "You expect Hank Gibson to drop whatever he's doing and rush over here to have a look at your car?"

"He'll come."

"Miss, for a stranger in town you're taking a lot for granted," Jason St. Clair informed her. "How about giving me the keys and letting me try?"

Pam never would have believed herself capable of glaring at Jason St. Clair, but she glared at him now. "For your information," she retorted coldly, "I am not a stranger in town. I've been around Bryant Lake most of my life."

Jason St. Clair held out a long slender hand, a hand Pam had watched accomplish all sorts of miracles on TV. As Griffith McQueen, he performed delicate, life-saving surgery on patients otherwise doomed to die. He'd also made exquisite love to several women, paramount among them Angela Santoro.

But what that hand wanted from her was her car keys. Pam gritted her teeth, handed them over and prayed he'd fail in his attempt to start her car. But of course he didn't. After a moment, the engine caught and revved smoothly.

Jason St. Clair got out of the car and said, "Maybe it was only flooded. Then again, maybe a tune-up and a new battery would be a good idea. Now, if you don't mind..."

"I'll move it," Pam said, without even looking at him.

She closed the heavy car door with a loud thump, then hit the gas hard enough to spray gravel before she backed around to the front of the store. There, fuming, she watched Jason St. Clair drive calmly off in his red Trooper and make a left turn on Main Street.

Inside the store again, Pam retrieved her milk, picked up a carton of diet tonic, then went back to the counter.

Bert Cullum was sorting through a pile of receipts. He looked up, and asked mildly, "What was the problem?"

"My blasted car wouldn't start...for me. It finally started for your Mr. Martin." She emphasized the phony name. "I thought I was parking back of Chris's car or I wouldn't have blocked the driveway."

"I guess Paul Martin told you he bought the car from Chris last week before Chris went back to school?"

Paul Martin, was it?

"Yes," Pam said.

"Chris had a chance to get a sports job cheap. Martin wanted a four-wheel drive vehicle like the Trooper so he could explore some of the mountain roads around here."

"What's he doing here?" Pam asked abruptly.

"Martin? He owns a cottage on the lake. Just a ways down from your place, in fact."

Pam stared at Bert suspiciously. "Since when?"

"Bought it about three years ago, if I remember right. Mostly uses it off-season. Sometimes comes up in the dead of winter."

"His place has heating?"

Bert shrugged. "He has a wood stove and a couple of space heaters. Says they do fine."

"Any idea where he's from?"

"Connecticut. He owns a company near New London that makes stuff for computers. Don't ask me exactly what. He told me, but I don't remember."

"Is he here by himself?"

The question came out a little sharper than Pam intended, and Bert looked at her curiously.

"That's why he comes here, Pam. To be by himself. To get away from the rat race, as he puts it." Bert was loading her purchases into a brown paper bag as he spoke. "Nice guy," he commented.

Pam sidestepped an answer and asked, "How much do I owe you?"

"Let's see . . . nine dollars and thirty-five cents."

Pam was about to fish in her handbag for some money when Bert said mildly, "You gave me a ten a few minutes ago, Pam. Here's your change."

"Thanks," Pam said hastily, and headed out into the blazing sunlight.

She was tempted to stop at Hank's garage and ask him to check out her car, but decided not to when it started on the first try. She wanted to get home and put the milk in the refrigerator, for one thing. She wanted to sit out on her porch overlooking the lake and try to relax.

She'd realized the lake wouldn't be completely deserted when she'd made the decision to come up. She'd expected to find a few campers and fishermen around during the lull between Labor Day and fall, when two or three weeks of magnificently colored foliage attracted an influx of tourists.

Generally speaking, though, she'd expected the kind of solitude along her stretch of the lake that would give her the chance to plunge into the project she was finally ready to tackle, without distraction. That's what she'd looked forward to, what she'd wanted.

So the idea that Jason St. Clair was living within a long stone's throw of her sadly dented her equilibrium. His presence on her horizon washed out her hope of having this beautiful place to herself while she tried to sort out the tangled skein her life had become and to get some work done.

Pam didn't doubt that Jason St. Clair wanted privacy as much as she did, or he wouldn't be here under an alias. But that didn't make her feel any more comfortable about having him so close.

What about his island retreat in Antigua? Or his ski lodge in Colorado? Weren't they private enough for him?

Pam settled into her cherished blue wicker rocker and looked across the lake's cobalt water to the dense pine forest that fringed the far shore. A state forest—nothing would ever be built there. Beyond the woods, rolling mountains sloped toward the sky. The nearest, Lyon's Peak, was as familiar to her as the palm of her hand. She and her father had climbed the trails so many times, years ago....

Her eyes misted. She'd known it would be traumatic to return to Bryant Lake, but she thought that time had eased her sorrow enough so that the pleasure would outweigh the pain. In a sense, that was so. It was wonderful beyond belief to be sitting in this rocker looking out on the scene she loved most in all the world. But she was intensely conscious of the empty rocker that stood just a couple of feet away.

Though four years had passed since her father's heart had given out, Pam's grief was suddenly as raw as a fresh wound. Tears streamed down her face and she gave vent to them, sobbing uncontrollably, letting out emotions that had been pent up for much too long. Sniffing, she finally had to go inside and get a handkerchief from the bedroom dresser. She was mopping her face dry when she heard the thumping on the front door.

Pam ignored the knocking at first. She didn't want to face anyone right now. Unfortunately, her car, parked to the side of the cottage, was a giveaway. Nevertheless, she thought resentfully, whoever was pounding at her door with such insistence might pause to think that maybe she was swimming, or had gone for a hike.

Such thoughts evidently weren't occurring. And, to Pam's presently oversensitive ears and jangled nerves, the door-pounding sounded hard enough to splinter the wood at any second. Irked, she flung the door open. And confronted Jason St. Clair.

He was holding an envelope by one corner as if it were something he couldn't wait to get rid of. He looked irritated and hot in the bargain. His sweat-soaked blue shirt clung to his chest, revealing the well-conditioned muscles that always looked so enticing on TV.

He'd changed his chinos for shorts. Pam saw legs she remembered only too well from one scene on *When Tomorrow Comes* where Griffith McQueen, M.D. had been presiding at a Fourth of July barbecue for the hospital staff.

She tore her eyes away from the blatantly disturbing aspects of Jason St. Clair's physique, and honed in on his face. He looked like a thundercloud. She saw none of the charismatic charm that came across in his role on the soap. Even so, he was incredibly handsome. Regardless of the tinted glasses, the need for a shave and the tousled hair, he had an undeniable basic appeal guaranteed to affect women of all ages.

Pam didn't see how he could possibly think he could go anywhere incognito with the hope of remaining unrecognized. Jason St. Clair was . . . unforgettable.

Yet somehow he'd managed to remain unrecognized here at Bryant Lake off and on for at least three years. For if anyone around had discovered that Paul Martin was really Jason St. Clair, it would be Bert Cullum. The general-store owner knew everyone in town, and everything that went on in this whole region.

Suddenly it dawned on her why Jason St. Clair had retained his anonymity in Bryant Lake. The television reception in the area was terrible; she had never encountered worse TV anywhere.

There were cable companies in both Newport to the west and St. Johnsbury to the south, but neither extended their services to this relatively remote and isolated section of the state. There just wasn't enough year-round population to justify the expansion. Most of the local Vermonters considered satellite-dish antennas prohibitively expensive, so they were few and far between. Only two channels came in, both from the nearby province of Quebec where the broadcasts were all in French. And as long as the situation continued, Jason St. Clair could hardly have found a safer escape hatch.

Now he stood just outside the door and stared down at Pam from what seemed like an imposing height. She remembered reading that he was six-two. She was five-six. At the moment, the eight-inch difference seemed like a mile.

"So...it *is* you," he observed. "I didn't think there'd be two cars exactly like yours around here. I take it you're also P. Martin?"

God, had he recognized her after all?

She shrank back. "Yes. Why?"

He held out the envelope. "This is for you."

"For me?"

"The letter was in my mailbox when I got back from the store. My name's Martin. Your name's Martin. Our first initials are both P. I live in the next cottage up the lake. Evidently the mail carrier mixed us up." He spoke patiently, as if he were explaining something to a confused child.

"What a coincidence," Pam managed to say. "Our having the same names, that is."

"Mmm," he agreed, his frown deepening. "If the mix-up continues I'll go into the post office and see if I can straighten it out. Meantime, I guess we should alert our correspondents to use our first names when they write."

Pam nodded, and took the envelope from him. She was about to thank him for bringing it over when he observed suddenly, "You've been crying."

Pam clutched the envelope with one hand and brushed her other hand over her cheeks. Despite her efforts with the handkerchief, they were still damp. She was sure her eyes were red-rimmed, too, and her nose probably looked like a ripe tomato. She didn't cry often, but when she did the results were not becoming. She could in no way rival the way Angela Santoro managed to weep and stay beautiful.

Jason St. Clair looked at her as if he were genuinely concerned. For a magic moment, Pam felt as though she were being given a brief, personal glimpse of Griffith McQueen, M.D. in action.

"Is something wrong?" he asked.

"Memories," Pam murmured, then wished she'd had the sense to hold her tongue.

"Memories?" His expressive brows lifted in tempo with his question.

"This is the first time I've been back to Bryant Lake for quite a while."

He nodded. "I knew I hadn't seen you around here before."

She waited apprehensively. Was he about to realize that though he'd never seen her around Bryant Lake, he *had* seen her elsewhere?

Evidently not.

"It's been four years since I last was here," she admitted.

"This cottage has been unoccupied all that time? I could have sworn there've been people here now and then."

"I've let friends borrow the cottage occasionally," she explained. "Aside from that, Bert Cullum's kept an eye on things for me. Made sure the pipes were drained so they wouldn't freeze in winter. Aired the place out in spring and summer. That sort of thing."

Jason St. Clair chuckled. "Bert *is* the guiding force around Bryant Lake, isn't he?"

Pam smiled despite herself. "I'd say so, yes."

"I learned early on that Bert's the man to go to if you want to know anything about anything around here."

"Or anyone," Pam added, without thinking.

Did she imagine it, or did a wary look creep into Jason St. Clair's eyes? Whatever, he started to back off.

Pam held his attention by indicating the envelope. "Thanks for bringing this over."

"You're quite welcome." He moved away, then abruptly turned. "Sure you're okay?" he asked.

"Yes," she said, surprised. "Why?"

"It's too bad your vacation started on a sad note, that's all. I take it the memories are sad?"

"Very sad, but also very happy," Pam found herself confessing. "I used to come here with my father. We shared a lot of wonderful hours in this place. This is my first time back since his death."

A strange expression flickered over Jason St. Clair's handsome face. For a moment Pam thought he was about to say something, but evidently he thought better of it.

"Well . . . take care," he said. And left, heading back up Pam's dirt driveway toward the road that passed along this side of the lake.

Pam closed the door gently, then leaned against it. Had Jason St. Clair really just hand-delivered a letter to her?

She glanced at the envelope. The letter was from her best friend, Linda Bailey.

She could imagine what Linda was writing to her about. Something that could wait. She was upset enough without adding fuel to the fire.

Pam supposed Jason St. Clair could have taken the letter up to Cullum's General Store and asked Bert to give it to her next time he saw her. It had been decent of him to bring it around himself. But his actions didn't mean he wanted his privacy invaded. For that matter, neither did she.

Chapter Two

Toward the middle of the afternoon, Pam put on a swimsuit and trekked down the path from her porch to the lake to take her first dip since coming back. The water, as she expected, was chilly. The initial icy shock went right through her. But then she swam fast and furiously, and after a few minutes her body began to adjust to the cold.

Her father had taught her to swim in Bryant Lake when she was a toddler, and he'd kept instructing her over the years so that she'd constantly improved her stroke. As a result, she was a strong swimmer. A little out of practice just now, but swimming was a skill one didn't forget.

She stretched each arm as she cut through the water, kicked steadily and concentrated on getting her breathing in sync. It was invigorating, perfect, so *exactly* what she needed.

The lake was two miles long, a half mile wide. Out of habit, Pam swam to her left, a course she'd followed ever since she could remember. She had no intention of doing a marathon swim this first time out. Still, she swam a good quarter mile before she decided to turn around. Halfway back, she relaxed and treaded water for a few minutes, charging herself up for a sprint swim back to the cottage. Then she saw Jason St. Clair.

He came out of his cottage, headed for the water, dove in, then struck out in her direction.

Only two people in a whole lake, dammit, and Jason St. Clair was bearing down on her like a torpedo. Unless she reversed directions or headed straight out toward the middle of the lake, a collision course seemed inevitable.

Pam swam this way, then that way, intending to give him as wide a berth as possible. But no matter how she maneuvered, he seemed to be coming directly toward her, cleaving through the water, turning his head to the side every four strokes to gulp in air without breaking his pace.

Then he stopped and started to tread.

And saw Pam, only fifteen feet away.

Though they were in a large lake with no one else around, Pam thought they looked like a couple of people who'd unavoidably come upon each other on a busy street corner—to their mutual displeasure.

"Miss Martin?" Jason St. Clair asked uncertainly.

"Yes," Pam answered. Was he having a problem recognizing her for the second time in just a few hours?

"I thought it was you," he muttered.

Who else? Pam wondered.

"This is the first time I've met anyone else swimming in the lake," he observed, as if wondering why this had to happen.

"You must stick to the off-season," she replied, her voice as cool as his. "How long have you been up here?"

"This time? Ten days. I drove up from New—" He broke off, then said carefully, "From New London."

Pam hoped her face didn't mirror her skepticism.

"What about you?" he asked. "When did you arrive?"

"Day before yesterday."

"Where from?"

"Boston."

He looked slightly uneasy. Maybe he was thinking that she might recognize him, especially without those slightly tinted glasses.

"Do you work?" he asked next.

The question confirmed Pam's suspicion. Possibly he was reasoning that if she worked she wouldn't be a fan of *When Tomorrow Comes*.

"Yes," she said, and didn't amplify.

"Just here for a short holiday?" he suggested.

She caught the hopeful note in his voice, and couldn't help feeling miffed. He didn't have to make it quite so plain that he'd love to see the last of her.

"I'm going to be here at least through October," she announced.

"Oh."

The single word said it all, and Pam was annoyed. Nettled, she asked, "How long are *you* going to be here?" She hoped he'd get the inference that she didn't relish his being around any more than he liked the idea of her proximity.

Jason St. Clair's face lost all expression, giving the effect of a window shade being drawn. "I'll be here indefinitely," he said. And without another word swam past her and struck out toward the far end of the lake.

Pam swam slowly back to shore. She felt chilled, both physically and emotionally, even after she toweled herself dry in the warm afternoon sunshine. Back in her cottage, she took a hot shower and slipped on a terry lounger. Only then did she begin to relax and feel warmer.

She took a cup of tea out on the porch and sipped while she scanned the lake, looking for a solitary swimmer. She thought of getting out the binoculars her father had always kept in a desk drawer in the living room. Probably they were still there, but using binoculars to track down her reclusive neighbor seemed an unfair advantage.

Instead, she depended on her natural vision, and finally Jason St. Clair came within its range. First he appeared as a tiny form moving slowly and steadily in her direction. Then he was like a distant figure in a photo as he made for shore and left the water for the sanctuary of his cottage.

He was shadowed, in silhouette, as he walked from the water's edge to his house. Even so, there was something about the way he walked that struck Pam unexpectedly. He looked . . . lonely. She couldn't have said what it was about him that gave that impression, only that he looked as lonely as she suddenly felt.

But loneliness or no loneliness, Jason St. Clair was here in Bryant Lake for a definite reason. Obviously he wanted to be alone.

Pam was so conscious of his evident wish to remain isolated that the next day she avoided doing some of the things she'd ordinarily have done. Like going for a long walk in the late afternoon along the shore. Or sauntering up the road past his cottage to a hillside spring where you could fill a jug with cool, clear, delicious water.

Instead, she stayed close to home. Which was easy enough because on the following day it rained. Now and then she glanced toward the telephone, and by midafternoon she was almost ready to call someone up just to hear the sound of another human voice. But she didn't.

If she called anyone she'd only be inviting questions she didn't want to answer.

She'd finally read Linda's letter and wished Linda had never written it.

Linda, an account executive at Jennings and Beverly Advertising and Public Relations, worked closely with Alfred Beverly, thus Alfred's moods affected her. Alfred was the more active of the two partners in the agency. Francis Jennings, the older partner, had been taking it easy in the wake of thoracic surgery.

Alfred, Linda complained in her letter, was being a bear—the direct result of Pam leaving Boston and refusing to tell him where she was going. He was being especially nasty to her, Linda complained, because it was she who'd introduced Pam to him.

It was these mood swings of Alfred's that only added to Pam's doubts about marrying him.

After reading the letter, Pam thrust it into the top desk drawer and tried not to think about it.

Finally the rainy day turned into an even rainier night. Pam showered and slipped into bed, still brooding about Alfred. She wanted to get married, she wanted to have kids, and Alfred was a good husband-father candidate. He was attractive, successful and could be great when he wanted to be. But the problem, she was learning, was that everything had to go his way or he wouldn't play.

She'd come here without telling him where she was going because she didn't want him to follow her. She needed to be by herself while she went through her father's journal. She was beginning a proposal for a book based on the journal for a small but distinguished publisher in western Massachusetts.

And she needed time away from Alfred so she could assess her real feelings about him, and what her future with him would be like if she yielded to his demand for a Christmas wedding.

Pam was lying in bed listening to the rain pattering down on the roof as, for the hundredth time in the past couple of days, she thought seriously about being married to Alfred. He was forty-two and tired of being a bachelor. He wanted to settle down, have a well-ordered life. Almost, but not quite.

That was another problem, and a big one. Before she could let Alfred slip a diamond on her finger, she had to be a lot more certain about her potential feelings for him than she was right now.

Pam had a sudden vision of Jason St. Clair as he'd looked in the middle of the lake—dark, sensual, his wet hair slicked back, water dripping down his handsome face, his eyes as silvery as rain would be if it could be bathed by a little bit of moonlight.

If a woman were in love with someone like Jason St. Clair, she wouldn't have to analyze her feelings. She'd *know*. There'd be no doubts, no questions. Love would be self-evident, warm, wonderful, passionate. A woman would melt in Jason St. Clair's arms, learn the meaning of ecstasy as she was caressed by him.

At least...that would be the case if the woman in question were dealing with Jason St. Clair as Griffith McQueen, M.D. Would the same hold true with Jason St. Clair as Paul Martin?

The question was unanswerable, because answering it would require a certain amount of experimentation. And, fortunately, there was no chance of any such experimenting taking place.

Jason St. Clair, or Paul Martin, was in Bryant Lake incognito. And even if he weren't...

Pam shut off her thoughts by forcing herself to concentrate on blackness. It took awhile for the blackness to begin to eclipse other visions. Then, finally, she turned on her side and fell asleep.

The rain stopped by morning but there were still clouds in the sky. It was almost noon before traces of blue began to weave through the gray. Pam, having run low on essential food supplies, drove into town and parked in front of Cullum's General Store. No more driveway problems, she promised herself.

A number of people in town had decided this was the right time to go shopping. Bert was busy, and Pam had no chance to talk to him. So she just picked up a few items and left.

Pam was nearing her cottage on the return trip when she saw Henry Beeman, who'd been driving the rural mail route ever since she could remember, stop at her mailbox, then drive on. She sighed. Another letter from Linda, undoubtedly, since Linda was the only person who knew where she was.

But it wasn't a letter from Linda. The envelope was white, business-size, and bore the imprint of a New York theatrical agency whose name she recognized. And it was addressed to "P. Martin, RFD #1, Bryant Lake, Vermont."

Pam took the letter in the house and put it on the kitchen counter while she set about unpacking the things she'd bought at Bert Cullum's. This chore finished, she eyed the envelope distastefully.

She needed either to deliver it to Jason St. Clair or to get in touch with him and ask him to pick it up. Did he have a telephone? She consulted the small Bryant Lake phone book, and saw there were only two Martins listed. Her phone was still under Joshua Martin, her father's name. The other Martin was Clarence, who ran the funeral home. I guess I'll have to deliver it, she thought.

Pam paused to survey her reflection in the bathroom mirror. She'd slept restlessly last night, and she looked it. There were shadows under her eyes. She didn't attempt to camouflage them—she wasn't in the mood to hide them with makeup—but she did put on a little lip gloss, then tried to brush her hair into some semblance of order. The damp weather had made her naturally curly hair even curlier.

She was wearing jeans again, and—since the rain had cooled the temperature down considerably—a lightweight blue sweater that enhanced the deep blue of her eyes. The sweater had shrunk a bit when she washed it so it was on the snug side, emphasizing the gentle swell of her breasts and stretching around her narrow waist.

Halfway to Jason St. Clair's cottage, she wished she'd changed the sweater for something looser, and nearly turned back. Then she told herself she was being silly. She was sure Jason St. Clair couldn't care less about what she was wearing. He couldn't even remember having seen her before.

His cottage was a little smaller than hers, but built of the same gray, weathered wood. Pam knocked on the front door and waited. Nothing happened. She knocked again. Then again. Then began to pound just as he'd pounded on her door the other day. The red Isuzu Trooper was parked beside the cottage. She knew damned well he was home.

She was right. He suddenly flung the door open, just as she'd flung her door open on him. She shrank from the expression she saw on his face. He looked down-right menacing. Then, as he recognized her, he relaxed slightly and said, "Yes?" But there was no welcome either on his face or in his voice.

Pam put on a smile and held out the envelope. "I'm afraid the mailman mixed us up again," she told him.

He took the envelope, and frowned as he surveyed the sender's name and address. "This is ridiculous," he began. "No point in bothering about it this afternoon, but first thing in the morning I'll visit the post office and try to get this straightened out."

"Lucky neither of us gets much mail," Pam quipped.

Jason St. Clair gave her a long, level glance, and she had the distinct impression he didn't think that was very funny. Then he said, "Regardless, I'll straighten it out."

Pam nodded, but she was only half listening to him. Her attention had been captured by something entirely different. Nestled at the edge of bushes that had been planted along the front of his cottage she saw a large, perfectly round white object.

"What is it?" Jason St. Clair asked, following her gaze.

"You've got yourself a *Calvatia gigantea,*" Pam murmured appreciatively. "Lucky you!"

"What are you talking about?"

"That puffball." She pointed. "It's a real treat."

"Puffball?"

"The giant mushroom." Pam nodded. "There, by that bush."

Jason St. Clair looked at it, and said direly, "I'll get rid of it."

"What do you mean, you'll get rid of it?"

"I'll throw it into the woods where it can rot."

Pam stared at him. "That would be sacrilege."

"Sacrilege? You're kidding, right?"

"No, I'm not. It so happens that *Calvatia giganteas* are precious. They may not be the rarest puffballs in the world, but they are considered choice. I wish I were lucky enough to find one at my place."

"Lucky enough?"

"That's right." She nodded. "*Calvatias* are absolutely delicious."

"You mean you'd eat that thing?"

"I wouldn't just eat it, I'd savor it."

"Then, by all means, be my guest. Take it home with you."

An inherent impishness in Pam, long suppressed, began to assert its rights. "I wouldn't think of doing that," she said demurely. "That is . . . I'd take it only if you allow me to fix half of it for you."

He stared at her as if he suspected she'd lost her mind. "I wouldn't touch a wild mushroom with a hundred-foot pole."

"Then you're really the loser."

He looked incredulous. "Are you serious?" he demanded. "Would you really eat a potentially poisonous mushroom?"

"What makes you think it's potentially poisonous?"

"Everyone knows wild mushrooms can kill you."

"Some of the wrong ones can," she agreed. "At least, they can make you pretty sick. But poisonous mushrooms aren't as commonplace as you might think. Nor is it all that hard to learn to tell the difference. My father took me mushrooming around here when I was a kid."

"Your father let you eat wild mushrooms?"

"*Safe* wild mushrooms, yes. Of course, you do have to know what you're doing."

"Of course," Jason St. Clair mimicked.

Pam met silver eyes that very briefly sparked with humor, but refused to let him get to her. "Some of the mushrooms that look like they might be the most dangerous are actually the safest," she told him. "You can't go by appearance. It might be that a mushroom with an outrageous shape and vivid color is a culinary delight, while another that looks pristine actually is deadly."

"Great," he muttered.

"Now, as for the *Calvatia*," Pam continued, her impish nature urging her on, "why don't you come over to my place and find out for yourself how good it is? If there's any danger at all, I won't cook it."

"How will you know?"

"Come and see," she invited sweetly.

He gave her a quick, suspicious look, but then he shrugged, and a faint smile tugged at the corner of his lips. "Why not? I admit you've made me curious. Of course, this might be my last lunch."

"I promise you it won't be."

"I'll try to believe you." He shut the front door behind him and came down the steps to her level.

Pam tenderly lifted up the huge puffball—nearly as large as a volleyball. Then she carried it carefully between her hands as they walked down the road to her place.

Her heart was pumping hard, a physical fact that had nothing to do with the *Calvatia*. She was overwhelmingly conscious of the man at her side. He was wearing his chinos again, and the casual comfortable look was perfect. His white sports shirt was open at the throat, giving an enticing glimpse of the curly dark tendrils on his chest. She caught a whiff of his scent, and it reminded her of the woods around the lake. Fresh and clean, but also quintessentially masculine. She was tempted to stumble just so he'd grasp her arm. She wanted to feel his touch on her skin; she wanted . . .

Pam swallowed hastily, and clutched her mushroom.

Once in her cottage, they made straight for the kitchen. She placed the puffball on the counter next to the sink, then reached in a drawer for a knife.

"Should be stainless steel," she informed her guest.

"I beg your pardon?"

"The knife. See, you slice straight down the middle. If the inside is pure white, you've struck treasure. If you see a dark shadow, you dispose of everything right away, then wash the knife with scalding water until there's no chance any poison is left." Pam told herself that, basically, she was telling him the truth. Just augmenting it with a little drama.

"Poison?" Paul echoed.

"Yes. If the inside is blackish, or purplish, this isn't a *Calvatia* and definitely isn't edible. If the inside reveals a dark mushroom shape, it could be the bud stage of something really deadly—which is why it's so important to thoroughly clean or even discard the knife, because you could be dealing with the dreaded 'Angel of Death.'"

That *was* laying it on a bit. But not too much, Pam decided, enjoying herself.

Jason St. Clair lifted both eloquent eyebrows and stared at the big white mushroom. "On second thought..." he began, "I'm not particularly keen on going any further with this."

"I wouldn't have anything further to do with the *Calvatia* myself if I were the least bit suspicious of it."

"Umm..." he said doubtfully. Then he smiled, and Pam felt as though her knees had turned to jelly. He'd shaved since the last time she'd seen him, his hair was still unruly, the clothes he wore faded and wrinkled. But he looked even more exciting right now than he did when he was starring as Griffith McQueen, M.D.

"I take it," he said lightly, still smiling, "you're not presently in a suicidal frame of mind?"

Pam's eyes widened. "What in the world would make you think that?"

"That," he said, pointing to the puffball. "Okay, I'll accept the fact that if you have any desire to continue living you wouldn't actually eat that without being sure about what you were doing."

"Thank you," Pam said with a mock bow. A thought struck her. "Look, why don't I pour us each a glass of white wine before I make the test? It might steady your nerves."

"Pour away," he invited.

Handing Jason St. Clair-alias-Paul Martin a glass of wine was like living out a fantasy. And when he clicked his glass to hers and toasted, "Here's to survival," Pam didn't even have to take a sip of the wine to feel as though it had already gone to her head.

When Jason-Paul smiled at her, she glowed. He made her feel warm and alive and desirable. Other men had indicated they'd found her desirable, but they'd never communicated this same kind of awareness. Pam felt as if the lake outside the windows had suddenly developed a tide that was carrying her along. And she wished the waves would lift her right into this man's arms.

She turned hastily and picked up the knife. "The moment of truth," she announced, and made a clean slice through the puffball. The two halves fell apart. Pam peered, then invited, "Look for yourself."

"Looks pure white," he announced.

"Pure white it is," she confirmed.

"So, what comes next?"

"I slice the *Calvatia* and fry it in butter while we sip our wine. I also happen to have a loaf of French bread in the freezer, which I'll pop in the oven. We really don't need anything more."

They didn't. When he'd finished the last bit of succulent, delicious mushroom, Paul—as Pam was trying to convince herself she must think of him—said, "I wouldn't have believed this. I've never tasted anything quite like it. Unique. That's the word for it."

"Yes. Unique," she agreed.

She leaned back, replete and happier than she'd been for a long time. Then she became aware that Paul— damn, but it was hard to think of him as Paul!—was looking at her closely. She wished the lenses of his glasses weren't tinted so she could see the expression in his eyes more clearly. As it was, his gaze was steady.

He said slowly, "You know, ever since I met up with you in Cullum's store I've had this feeling I've seen you somewhere before."

Pam felt as though her heart was about to stop beating.

Now, especially, she didn't want him to remember where he'd seen her. The memory would shatter this delightful experience.

She'd never forget the night, over a year and a half ago, when she'd been a guest on the popular TV game show, *Celebrity Circle,* and Jason St. Clair had been her celebrity partner.

She would never have chosen to go on the show of her own accord. In fact, she hadn't even been aware that there was a contestant search going on in Boston. Some of her co-workers had submitted her name because they were always teasing her about being a walking encyclopedia. Once she received the word that the staff of *Celebrity Circle* wanted to interview her, there was no way they'd let her back out.

What they'd done, really, was to throw down a gauntlet, and Pam had been damned if she'd back away from the challenge. So she'd appeared at Boston's Ritz-Carlton Hotel at four o'clock on a wintry Thursday afternoon, had been interviewed by the hosts of *Celebrity Circle* and was accepted as a contestant.

Then the night had come when she'd joined the other contestants in a New York TV studio. Before the show started, each contestant had been teamed up with a celebrity. When Pam discovered that Jason St. Clair was to be her partner, any answer to a question she might ordinarily have known flew right out of her head. It wasn't that long since she'd watched him on *When Tomorrow Comes.* But the reality of Jason St. Clair in the flesh had been even more overwhelming than the image he evoked on TV.

In addition, Pam had soon discovered she suffered from stage fright. There was a large live audience and, looking out at the sea of faces, she'd felt as though she'd suddenly developed a giant-size prune pit in the middle of her stomach.

Her feet literally turned cold. Her hands shook, so that she fumbled every time she was supposed to push a buzzer. Jason St. Clair tried to help her out, but the results were dismal. She'd been bested by a sixty-five-year-old housewife and an eighteen-year-old high school senior.

Jason St. Clair had been extremely kind as he consoled her in her defeat. Too kind. He couldn't have been smoother, or a better actor. Pam unwittingly sensed a mockery behind his charming facade, and couldn't wait to get away from him, rush out of the studio and escape back to her hotel.

Later, the sympathy of her colleagues at the *Record* had only made matters worse. They insisted she hadn't been all that bad—she'd consistently drawn the most difficult questions, that was all. But Pam felt certain that she'd come on as the dumbest contestant ever to appear on anyone's game show. Since then, she'd had a lot more sympathy and tolerance for people who had difficulty in projecting their personalities and expressing themselves, especially in difficult circumstances.

"What's the matter, Pam?" Jason-Paul asked her.

"N-nothing," she stammered.

He asked cautiously, "Do you feel like we've met somewhere before?"

Pam caught the anxiety in his voice and realized he was more worried than she was. He didn't want her to remember him, either...though for entirely different reasons than hers. Pam took mercy on him, and said, "I'd say our paths have never crossed."

That was true enough. Their paths had run parallel for a terrible half hour while they sat next to each other on *Celebrity Circle*. They hadn't actually met until she'd arrived here in Bryant Lake.

She saw Jason-Paul relax, and was glad she'd shaded the truth. No harm done, she thought, as she suggested another glass of wine and he accepted.

They spent the rest of the afternoon talking about a variety of things—all impersonal. Like collecting wild mushrooms. Discussing a book they'd both read. Discovering they both liked Greek food and Greek music.

As he lingered on her doorstep before leaving, Jason-Paul suggested, "My place next time?"

"That would be great," Pam said, trying to breathe evenly in an effort to keep her soaring pulse rate down.

"I can't promise anything as exotic as a *Calvatia*, but I do make a terrific moussaka," he told her. "The recipe," he added, "came straight from Athens."

"Marvelous."

And it would have been marvelous . . . the whole interlude at the lake might have been marvelous—Pam later reasoned bitterly—if she hadn't decided to go to St. Johnsbury on a shopping trip the next day.

Chapter Three

Pam went to St. Johnsbury with a single purpose in mind. She needed a new raincoat.

She found a bright orange slicker in a discount store, and was in line at the checkout counter when she spotted the bold headline of one of the tabloid papers stacked in the magazine rack.

Where is Jason St. Clair? she read. Under the banner a second headline stated, Star of *When Tomorrow Comes* Has Disappeared.

Pam reached for the paper, saw that the main story was on page two, turned to it and began to read.

Jason St. Clair, American's heartthrob male soap-opera star—a man who makes women across the country wish they had medical problems so that they could be treated by Griffith McQueen, M.D.—has seemingly vanished from the face of the earth.

St. Clair was last seen at his New York City residence nearly two weeks ago. Bill McGillicuddy, a doorman at the actor's exclusive East Side condo, remembers calling for St. Clair's custom Jaguar coupe to be brought around to the front entrance. According to McGillicuddy, nothing seemed out of the ordinary when the actor drove off alone.

He hasn't been seen or heard from since.

Is St. Clair in hiding? Is he trying to escape from the Thanksgiving wedding his costar, Angela Santoro, reputedly is planning? His hideaway estates in Antigua and in Aspen, Colorado, have been checked out, to no avail. There have been unconfirmed sightings of St. Clair in Lisbon, on the Adriatic coast, Hawaii and Anchorage. But coworkers are saying St. Clair may have met with an accident, or worse.

The possibility that St. Clair may have suffered an injury, or is stricken with amnesia, has surfaced. According to a source who spoke on the condition his name not be used . . .

Pam became aware that the checkout clerk was giving her a very cold eye. She rummaged in her handbag for money, paid for her purchase and walked away with the tabloid tucked under her arm.

Back at her car, she settled down to read the whole account. Angela Santoro was described as being close to collapse, and in seclusion in her West End apartment. Thus far, the actress had refused to be interviewed and wouldn't even make a statement.

The police were investigating the possibility of foul play. Nor could suicide be ruled out. There was speculation about whether St. Clair had seemed depressed lately. Other members of the cast of *When Tomorrow Comes* said it was the star's policy to keep pretty much to himself.

"Jason's always been a loner," the actor who plays Evan Parker, Chief of Surgery at Anderson-Gorman General Hospital, was quoted as saying. "Usually when he's working, he's low-key, easy to get along with. But off the set he maintains a private profile."

Actually, St. Clair has been "off the set" since the show resumed taping after the summer hiatus—but this, according to Jerry S. Bernstein, St. Clair's agent, is because the episodes for the new season began with the show's star written out of the script.

"There's nothing so unusual in that," Bernstein insisted at a press conference yesterday. "The current story line takes place during a brief leave of absence Griffith McQueen has taken in order to fly on a mercy mission to a village in Central America. The casualty toll in an earthquake was heavy, people are urgently in need of the services of skilled surgeons. McQueen has flown to the stricken village to save lives."

"Although not working on the set so far this season, St. Clair was in town until two weeks ago," Bernstein said. He added that St. Clair's subsequent absence from the Manhattan scene has nothing to do with impending contract negotiations between the star and the producers of the show.

Bernstein insisted that his "gut feeling" is that St. Clair is okay and will soon show up. "I think he just needed a little time to himself," Bernstein told reporters.

Pam could relate to a need for private time. And Jerry Bernstein, she suspected, was the one person who knew where the TV star was and what he was doing. JSB Ltd. had been the return address on that envelope she'd given Jason.

Paul, she amended.

She had to smile. Evidently she and Jason-Paul each had just one person in their lives whom they really trusted. Jason-Paul had his agent. She had Linda Bailey.

Let's hope neither of them caves in under pressure, Pam prayed silently.

There was more to the tabloid story—background information on Jason St. Clair, plus sidebars quoting fans on the street. She decided she'd read the rest later. She put the paper aside and started back to Bryant Lake. But she was troubled as she drove.

There were pictures of Jason St. Clair accompanying the stories, as well as photos of Angela Santoro and others in the soap-opera cast. To Pam, the resemblance between Jason St. Clair and Paul Martin was unmistakable, despite Paul's tinted glasses and shaggy hair. If someone else from Bryant Lake ventured over to St. Johnsbury to shop, or spotted the tabloid elsewhere, Jason-Paul's time out of the limelight might be over.

She wished she knew why he was so intent on attempting to vanish from the face of the earth. Judging from surface appearances, anyone would think he had it all: looks, fame, fortune, and the devotion of an extraordinarily beautiful woman. Nevertheless, it stood to reason that he wouldn't be hiding out in a remote corner of northern Vermont without a strong motivation.

Maybe just the need to escape, to get out of the public eye for a while, was motivation enough, Pam mused. Maybe Jason-Paul's motivation was even stronger. Speculating on that, Pam experienced a familiar itch. Her journalistic nose was twitching. The habits of a lifetime didn't die easily, she thought ruefully. Her father had instilled that nose for news in her at an early age, and there was no use pretending she could be disinterested in a headline story.

On the other hand, she was not at Bryant Lake as a columnist-reporter. She'd come—on leave of absence from the *Record*—to try her hand at a full-length book. If she succeeded with the book to be based on her father's journal, she might decide to take the plunge, resign from her job at the paper and free-lance.

Pam glanced toward the tabloid. How her father would have deplored that type of journalism. His newspapers had maintained a high standard of integrity. He had hated sensationalism. At the same time, he'd never turned his back on a good story.

Joshua Martin, she thought proudly, had built up his newspaper empire by sheer hard work and by sticking to his code of ethics. His "empire" had been relatively small—he'd never attempted to rival the industry giants like Gannett or Hearst. But his papers had been noted for their editorial excellence, and had won many coveted awards.

Joshua had started with a daily paper in western Massachusetts. By the time Pam was in college, Martin Publications owned six papers in different New England cities. Summers, she worked on one or another of her father's papers, except for the times when she and

Joshua escaped to Bryant Lake, the place they both loved the most.

Her mother had died when she was two. Joshua, Pam remembered sadly, had never fallen in love again. He had divided the waking hours of his life—which outnumbered those when he slept by at least four to one—between his newspapers and his daughter.

Neither of them had ever had any doubt that once Pam was out of college she'd become a reporter for Martin Publications. She loved journalism, and she'd known that no one would ever accuse her father of nepotism if she went to work for him. Matter of fact, she'd had to work harder than the other reporters, and turn in better copy, to prove her worth.

Then, she recalled sadly, just a few months after she'd joined Martin Publications, Joshua suffered his first coronary. Soon he was told by his doctors that he had two choices: stay in the saddle and die before his time, or take an early retirement.

He'd taken the second option—because of Pam. She'd known that at the time, and still was painfully aware that her father had given up the work he loved for her sake.

Unfortunately, the sacrifice hadn't paid off. Within a year of selling out, Joshua Martin was dead.

Meantime, the large conglomerate that bought Martin Publications wanted Pam to keep her job. But she soon discovered she didn't like working for the new owners. Their ideas were a world apart from the journalistic concepts on which she'd been brought up. Not as bad as the tabloid at her side, but bad enough.

Four years ago, she'd decided to take a summer-long respite, then look for a job on another paper come fall. She would forever be thankful that she'd made that decision. She and her father had spent the beautiful weeks of summer here at Bryant Lake. Those were the last weeks they'd shared together, and the memory of that time was priceless.

Pam brushed away the heavy sorrow that threatened to engulf her, and thoughts of Jason-Paul resurfaced.

Admittedly, her nose for news was quivering. She smiled, thinking how her father would react to her discovery that her reportorial instincts just couldn't be squelched. But then the smile faded as she seriously considered the scoop she was sitting on.

She tried to tell herself that her paper didn't go in for tabloid-type sensationalism. Her editor wouldn't be all that interested in a story on Jason St. Clair-alias-Paul Martin. Would he?

Who are you kidding, Martin? Pam asked herself, as she drove down her sloping driveway and parked beside the cottage.

She sat in the car for a minute, staring out at the lake. A good story was a good story. She'd stumbled onto an intriguing story—but she knew she couldn't write it.

There was such a thing as decency. A person like Jason-Paul had a right to privacy when he craved it, enough to stage such an elaborate disappearing act. Pam got out of the car, carrying the tabloid and her new rain slicker, and told herself Jason-Paul should be able to do exactly what he was doing.

His secret would be safe with her.

She put the tabloid on the desk in the living room, and was just putting away her new slicker when she heard a loud thump on her front door.

Jason-Paul? Pam hoped so. And her wish was granted.

The man who was claiming such a large measure of her thoughts stood on her doorstep, looking anything but happy.

Had he somehow seen the tabloid? Bert Cullum only carried local newspapers and a limited selection of magazines. The pharmacy in Bryant Lake stocked out-of-town newspapers, more magazines and paperbacks. Neither store handled material like the tabloid. Pam couldn't think of any place short of St. Johnsbury where you could get one of the papers. Even so...

"I have a favor to ask," Jason-Paul said abruptly.

Pam smiled. "Ask away."

"May I use your phone? I've never wanted a phone in my cottage, but unfortunately I need to make a call. I'd use the phone booth in Cullum's Store, but...it's awfully public."

"By all means, use the phone. It's on the desk. I was about to make some coffee. Would you like a cup?"

"That would be good." Jason-Paul spoke absently.

He started for the desk as Pam started for the kitchen. She was almost at the kitchen door when she remembered the tabloid. She swung around with the vain hope that maybe she could rush over and snatch it before he saw it. But the hope was doomed.

Jason-Paul picked up the tabloid, and Pam saw him stiffen. His eyes flickered over the headlines. He turned the page, and she held her breath as she realized he was staring at pictures of himself. Then he looked across at her, and—despite the tinted glasses—she felt her skin being seared.

"Where did you get this?" he demanded.

"In...St. Johnsbury," she stammered.

"Is this on sale anywhere in town?"

"In Bryant Lake? No, I'm sure it isn't."

He dropped the tabloid on the desk as if its pages might contaminate him, and muttered a couple of expletives that Griffith McQueen, M.D. would *never* have thought of using.

"I guess my attempt at a disguise has been pretty sorry, hasn't it?" he asked bitterly. And, with a glance at the tabloid, added, "You don't have to say anything. The look on your face tells me you recognized me in those pictures, right?"

"Yes."

"But this doesn't come as news to you, does it?" There was anger in his voice.

"What makes you say that?"

"Don't hedge, Pam. I've had a funny feeling about you ever since that day in Cullum's store. I'm right, am I not? This doesn't come as news to you?"

"No," Pam admitted.

"How long have you known?"

"How long? Well, I . . ."

"Come off it, Pam!" he commanded. "You knew who I was the minute you first saw me, didn't you?"

She nodded slowly. "Yes."

"Why the hell didn't you say so? Then, or later?"

She swallowed. "It seemed obvious that you wanted to be . . . incognito."

He scowled. "You're damn right I wanted to be incognito. And I've had no problem keeping my so-called identity under wraps here in Bryant Lake until now. Before I bought the cottage, I investigated the whole area."

"Investigated?"

Jason-Paul nodded. "Bryant Lake has the worst television reception of anyplace in New England. The geography, the isolation . . . it doesn't matter, the TV around here is lousy. From what I could come up with, there aren't many places in the entire country where it's much worse."

He surveyed her coldly. "Bryant Lake has been the ideal spot for me to go around like an ordinary person," he stated. "No hassles, no reporters, no photographers poking their cameras into my face every time I step outside."

"And you think I'm going to blow your cover?"

He laughed shortly. "You've been reading too many spy stories. But since you put it that way, what else am I supposed to think?"

"As far as I know," Pam said carefully, "no one else around Bryant Lake is aware of your true identity. If Bert Cullum doesn't know who you really are, I'd say your secret's safe. Then again, you do look . . . quite different from the way you look on TV. The phony glasses, for one thing—"

"The glasses are not phony," he said tightly. "Maybe the tinted lenses are intended as a sort of camouflage, but I need the glasses. I'm nearsighted. That's why I wasn't sure it was you swimming out in the lake the other day until I was practically on top of you."

"Oh," Pam said. And couldn't resist adding, "But on *When Tomorrow Comes* . . ."

"I wear contacts," he interjected. "You couldn't imagine Griffith McQueen, M.D. wearing *glasses,* could you?" The question dripped sarcasm. "Damn him," Jason-Paul concluded resentfully.

Pam's curiosity was brimming over. Mixed with it was a compassion she hadn't expected to feel. She was aware of this man's insidious attractiveness, but right now he looked like someone who'd lost his last friend. She yearned to throw her arms around him and promise she wouldn't reveal his secret, and be close by when he needed her....

Pam stopped herself short. Who did she think she was? Angela Santoro?

With an effort, she steadied herself. "Look," she said, "I'm not about to blab, if that's what's worrying you."

"No?" he asked skeptically. "What about this?"

"What about what?"

He hoisted a large brass paperweight from a corner of the desk. "Martin Publications," he read. "An award for journalistic excellence. I take it there's a connection between Martin Publications and Pamela Martin?"

Pam flushed. "My father owned Martin Publications."

"Ah."

"Don't say it like that. My father sold his newspapers to the Chalmer chain several months before he died."

"The plot thickens," Jason-Paul observed ironically.

"No, the plot doesn't thicken," Pam contradicted. "It thins."

"Can you honestly tell me you have no connection with the Chalmer papers?"

That was easy. "I have no connection with the Chalmer papers," Pam said steadily. Before he could comment, she added, "And if you're still wondering whether I'm about to sell you out, the answer is no. Now...why don't you make your phone call, and I'll put on a pot of coffee."

Pam stalked off to the kitchen and deliberately closed the door. She hoped that would convince Jason-Paul that she had no intention of eavesdropping on his conversation.

After a few minutes he opened the door and came into the kitchen so quietly that she jumped.

"You startled me," she complained.

"Sorry."

Again, Pam felt his silvery eyes sear her.

Her hand shook slightly as she filled two mugs with coffee. "Let's go out on the porch," she suggested. Suddenly, the cottage seemed too small to hold both Jason-Paul and herself.

He shrugged indifferently. "If you like."

Pam led the way and settled into the blue rocker. She watched Jason-Paul take the other rocker, and for a moment it seemed very odd to see a man other than her father sitting in that chair. Yet it also seemed right. The chair had been empty long enough.

She became sharply aware of how much she needed a man in her life. Not a father figure, she amended hastily. She'd had the most wonderful father a person could possibly have. She wasn't looking for a surrogate parent. She needed a man to share her life with, that's all. She needed the strength and comfort of a male presence.

No... in all honesty, she needed more than that. She needed a man to love, a man who would love her in return. She needed a man with whom she could *make* love. She knew intuitively that she had a great capacity for giving—if the right person were there to receive her gift. And when it came to finding the right person, she couldn't afford to make a mistake. Because the gift she had to offer was herself. All of her. And that was a gift that couldn't be given twice.

Jason-Paul said, "You're very quiet."

"I was just . . . thinking."

He nodded. "I've been doing some overtime thinking myself the past few minutes."

Pam waited for him to go on.

"That was my agent I called," he finally told her. "Jerry Bernstein, in New York. I wanted to talk to him about . . . other things. But the tabloid story takes precedence. He'd already seen it, need I say? He said they quoted him."

"Yes, they did."

"I told Jerry that a late journalist's daughter has discovered who Paul Martin really is."

"I don't like the way you say that," Pam muttered. "Jason St. Clair . . . Paul Martin . . . just what *is* your real name, anyway?"

For a second, the man sitting across from her looked as if she'd thrown him a curve. Then, he actually smiled. A sweet-sad smile that transformed the hard edges of his face.

"My real name is Paul Jason Martin," he told Pam. "The St. Clair was concocted as a stage name." He sipped his coffee, then asked curiously, "Just how did you recognize me so quickly? I really thought I looked like a local, or just another guy up for a week of fishing."

"Not to me."

Paul Jason Martin looked disgusted. "Then you *are* a follower of *When Tomorrow Comes.*" He shook his head. "God, they're everywhere."

"It wasn't the show," Pam said.

Paul's eyes became fixed on her face, his gaze so compelling it made her squirm.

"Okay," he said. "Where did we meet?"

"I . . ."

"Where did we meet, Pam?"

Pam discovered she couldn't tell him a deliberate lie. She said unhappily, "You and I were on television together about a year and a half ago."

"We were *what?*"

"I was a contestant on *Celebrity Circle.*"

Paul's brow furrowed. Then he said, "Now I know why I've felt all along that I'd seen you before." There was no triumph in the statement. "You were that girl in the purple dress."

Pam felt like throwing herself in the lake. "I'm afraid so."

"You looked ... very different." He scanned her closely. "You had on a ton of makeup, for one thing."

"I'd been told it was necessary because of the lights."

"Some, yes. But you'd really plastered on the paint. And your hair was different."

"I used a lot of mousse because I didn't want it flying all over the place."

"Another mistake," he commented. "You have beautiful hair. You should have let it fly all over the place. The effect is very becoming." He paused, as if remembering the episode more clearly, then said, "Oh, yes, and that dress you wore ..."

"I didn't know you were so observant," Pam cut in stiffly.

"I wasn't. It's just that the color socked me in the eye. It also diminished the effect of your natural coloring, washed you out despite all the extra makeup."

"I was told it was best to wear a bright color."

"It's best to wear what looks good on you," Paul advised, "as I'm sure a lot of bright colors do." He amended, more sympathetically, "Hey...I didn't mean to sound critical. Now that I think of it, your disguise was more effective than mine.''

''It wasn't a disguise.''

He shrugged. ''I knew something was funny when I ran into you at the general store. But I never would have connected you with the game show.''

Pam wondered if she looked as miserable as she felt. ''You don't remember my performance?'' she asked.

''Your performance?''

''I was terrible.''

''You're saying that because we lost?''

''We were crushed. Not because of you. It was all my fault. My mind went blank and I just about lost my voice at the same time.''

Paul actually chuckled. ''Funny you should feel you were responsible for our poor showing,'' he commented. ''I remember I blamed myself for our dismal performance. My mind was elsewhere that night. I realized you were a nervous wreck, but that didn't shake me out of my preoccupation. A hazard with dissatisfied actors,'' he finished.

He muttered the final sentence so that Pam had to strain to hear it. ''What do you mean, dissatisfied?'' she asked, puzzled.

His expression turned grim. ''Better you should ask what I mean by 'actor,''' he countered.

''I'm not following you.''

Paul rocked back and forth, his handsome face somber. ''I'm not an actor,'' he stated flatly. ''At least not a naturally gifted actor.''

Pam stared at him. ''How can you possibly say that? You're not only an actor, you're a star!''

''A manufactured star, built up by a lot of hype.''

"On the contrary, Griffith McQueen, M.D. is very convincing. He's warm and real—"

"So. . ." Paul accused, "you *have* seen the show."

"I saw it a couple of years ago, when I stayed home from work for three weeks with a bad case of flu."

"And you were hooked?"

"I. Well. . ."

"You were hooked," Paul said decisively.

Pam glared at him mutinously. "I was not hooked on the show. The story was really nothing special. . . ."

"But Griffith McQueen, M.D. was?"

Pam's glare intensified. Why was he taking such delight in embarrassing her?

He stopped rocking, and said soberly, "That's the problem, Pam. Nobody—no fan, or producer, or director—will even recognize me for me. Unless I do something drastic, I'm always going to be Griffith McQueen, M.D. Period."

"Is that so bad?"

"To me it is." Paul hesitated, then continued unhappily. "There's something about Griffith McQueen, M.D. that appeals to women. Something contagious that's pure fantasy."

"You make it sound worse than having the plague." Pam had to smile. "It can't be so terrible to have half the women in America fantasizing about you, can it?" she challenged.

Paul looked at Pam, and held her gaze. "It makes me want Griffith McQueen, M.D. dead."

Pam's jaw dropped. "You want him *dead?*"

"Right." He nodded. "Dead and buried. I want the writers to write him out of the script. Knock him off. Kill him. I don't care how they do it, I just want them to do it. No loopholes, no dream sequences, no chance whatsoever for a resurrection. He's off-camera now, in Central America. In my opinion, this is the perfect time to finish him off. I've fulfilled my contract and I'm damned if I'm going to sign a new one, despite the pressure the producers and my agent are putting on me. That's why I was temporarily written out of the script— because I saw to it that the producers and I couldn't come to terms before the new season started, no matter how hard Jerry tried to push me."

He stood. "I won't bore you with the business details," he said. "Suffice it to say that I don't want to go back to the show. I thought I'd made that pretty clear, but when I realized I hadn't made it clear enough I decided to leave town for a while. I want to force the show to do away with McQueen so I can get on with my life."

Pam shook her head. "I don't believe this. You can't mean what you're saying."

"I mean every word. That's why I'm here, why I hoped I could stay here without anyone finding out where I was until I convinced both Jerry and the producers that I'm not coming back. I'm aware this will probably be the kiss of death for me as far as getting jobs on television dramas is concerned, but I don't give a damn."

Pam could *feel* Paul's silvery gaze through the tinted lenses. The effect was distracting. She nearly missed what he said next, but then the echo of his words penetrated her consciousness.

"So," he told her, "you might as well add *that* to your story."

Pam sprang to her feet, her body responding like a coiled spring. She clenched her fists, moved a step in his direction and declared heatedly, "I told you I wouldn't sell you out. Don't you have any faith in anybody?"

He came closer, towering over her. "Not much," he admitted. "Also, I'm remembering now that on *Celebrity Circle* they said you were a journalist and you answered a couple of questions about your career. You say you have no connection with the Chalmer papers. Does that mean you've given up journalism?"

"No."

"Where do you work, Pam?"

"I'm a columnist for the *Boston Record*. I do some reporting, too, but I mostly work on slice-of-life stories."

"This would make a great slice-of-life piece, wouldn't you say?" Paul queried dryly.

"Damn you," Pam swore, "you really are jaundiced about people, aren't you? Why do you think I'm here at Bryant Lake? I know what it means to want peace and privacy. I know what it means to need to get away because you absolutely have to be alone to make decisions. I have to decide where my life's going just as much as you have to decide about yours. I have to make up my mind whether or not I'm going to get married and, regardless of marriage, what I'm going to do with my career. Believe me, you're not the only one who's ever gotten in a bind and can't find the way out. I . . ."

Pam's words were coming faster and faster.

She lost track of what she'd been about to say as two strong, slender hands clasped her shoulders. Stiffening, she looked up into Paul's handsome face, at the same time feeling as though his palms were burning holes in the fabric of her shirt.

"Hold it," he urged. "Just stop and think about this for a minute. You have me in your power, lady. What happens to me largely depends on the next move you make.

"No," he went on quickly as she started to speak, "don't say anything. Just accept the fact I realize the only choice I have right now is to try to trust you—and, believe me, it's not easy to contemplate trusting a member of the media. But it's either that or packing up and leaving here. And where else could I go?

"Think about that," Paul told Pam, then suddenly dropped his hands from her shoulders, turned and walked out her front door, carefully shutting it behind him.

Pam closed her eyes tightly, still seeing his troubled face, still breathing in his warm, masculine scent, spiced with woodsy after-shave. The sound of his mellow voice rang in her ears.

For a second, she'd had the crazy impression he was going to kiss her. Pam circled her lips with the tip of her tongue as if she could somehow savor the taste of him, even though the kiss hadn't come to pass.

She thought about what he'd said about her having him in her power. That, of course, was ridiculous. Or was it? She was the one who could call the shots right now, and she wouldn't have been human if that thought didn't give her a heady feeling. She could take this situation and weave a story just as dramatic as the script of *When Tomorrow Comes*.

Except, she realized suddenly, this wasn't Griffith McQueen, M.D. or Jason St. Clair she was dealing with. This was Paul Jason Martin.

This wasn't make-believe. This was real.

Chapter Four

Clouds blotted out the moon, so Pam hunted around for a flashlight before starting out for Paul's house. She thought about going along the beachfront, then opted to walk down the road, where the footing would be easier on a night like this.

Paul's living-room light was on, which was good, though she'd already made up her mind to pound on his front door till he responded even if the house was in darkness. She felt bone tired, but she knew there was no way she'd be able to get any rest tonight until she talked to him.

As she approached the house, she heard music and identified Mahler, her favorite classical composer.

Paul was so slow about coming to the door that Pam suspected he thought there were already reporters on his trail. Which signaled that she was right—he hadn't trusted her discretion.

"Oh, you person of little faith," she chided, just as he finally flung the door open.

Etched against the light in the room, he looked slightly larger than life, an effect that wasn't diminished when he flipped a switch near the door.

Pam blinked, the sudden light dazzling her eyes. Recovering, she glanced up at Paul and saw that he was watching her warily.

"What is it?" he asked.

"I have to talk to you." The admission made her uncomfortable.

He frowned. "Now?"

She nodded. "Yes." She added honestly, "Otherwise I won't be able to sleep."

She couldn't blame him for looking so skeptical. But he only said curtly, "Well, I'd hate to be the cause of your staying awake. Come in."

It wasn't a very gracious invitation, but what could she expect? Pam walked into his living room, accepting the fact that she was not the person he most wanted to see at the moment.

Who was? she wondered. Anyone?

People who knew Paul a lot better than she did—people who'd been quoted in stories about him—claimed he was a loner. Regardless...was there a chance there might be a significant other in his life? Someone beside Angela Santoro? Someone whom he'd been able to keep out of the publicity releases?

She doubted it. It stood to reason that if Paul had a significant other—aside from Angela—that person would be with him now in Bryant Lake. In her opinion, he needed both company and a confidante. But she was not about to delude herself into imagining she could qualify for either of those roles, let alone both of them.

Paul had made it abundantly clear that members of the media were poison to him.

Frustrated, Pam moaned, "Oh, *hell,*" under her breath.

She hadn't thought he could hear her, but he did. He turned quickly. "Did you say something?"

"Not really." She was looking around the room. The walls were pine-paneled, the furniture covered with chintzy slipcovers and there were pictures of dogs and horses on the wall.

He said, as if reading her mind, "It came this way."

She swung around. "What?"

"The cottage. I bought it furnished and I haven't done anything about it. I just want you to know that the decor doesn't necessarily reflect my taste, in case you decide to write your impressions in your story." As he spoke, Paul crossed the room and turned the volume down on a compact disc sound system. "This," he said, "is the only thing I've added to the cottage, thus far. You might want to make a note of that, too."

Damn the man!

Goaded, Pam snapped, "It would serve you right if I *did* do a story about you. Matter of fact, why don't you come back to my house with me? I'll phone my editor in Boston and you can listen in."

"Thank you, but no thank you."

She glared at him. "Do you trust *anyone?*"

She expected him to come back with a quick answer, but he took time to consider what she'd asked. Then he said slowly, "I guess I'd have to say I trust Jerry Bernstein. My agent. Jerry thinks I'm an idiot to leave *When Tomorrow Comes* while the show's so hot, especially when they're offering considerably more money if I'll sign a new contract. But he wouldn't let me down for the sake of his commission."

"How noble of him."

Paul chuckled. "I don't think Jerry could relate to the idea of being considered noble."

"Too bad for Jerry."

"Pam..."

"What?"

"Perhaps I *have* been misreading you."

"Is that doubt I hear in your voice?" She couldn't resist the sarcasm. "Are you beginning to think maybe I'm not going to toss you to all those voracious females waiting to gobble you up?"

He smiled. "I'm not so conceited as to believe there are a lot of hungry women out there waiting to devour *me*," he said. "But I have to admit there may be a fair number of them eager to get their talons on Griffith McQueen, M.D." He switched the subject quickly. "Why couldn't you go to sleep tonight without talking to me?"

"It...it doesn't matter." Pam knew she sounded flustered. She felt flustered. His smile was getting to her. She said unsteadily, "I'm sorry I butted in like this," and started for the door.

Paul's hand on her arm detained her. "Wait just a minute." He spaced the words out evenly. "Do you think I'm about to let you walk out of here on that note?"

Again, she felt as though his touch were scorching her. Damn...like all the other women around the country who followed him on TV, she was responding to him as she would to Griffith McQueen, M.D.

Griffith McQueen, M.D.? Pam admitted that she was deliberately trying to use fantasy as an out. Because the reality hitting her was so overpowering.

She wasn't reacting to Paul's alter ego right now, if that's what Griffith McQueen, M.D. could be called. She was reacting to Paul Martin, who without doubt was the most desirable man she'd seen in her entire life.

Her cheeks suddenly felt hot.

"I'm not letting you leave till you tell me why you came," he advised her. Then he queried logically, "If you couldn't get to sleep when you arrived here without talking to me, what makes you think you can now?"

Maybe he could be logical right now. She couldn't be. "Please . . ." Pam began.

"I mean it, Pam."

Pam sighed, straightened. "Okay," she said. "I'm upset because you won't believe me. That doesn't seem fair to me, and I . . . resent it. I guess I shouldn't blame you for not trusting journalists. I suppose if I were in your position I might feel the way you do about the media. But we're all different. *I'm* different."

When he didn't respond, she went on doggedly, "Look, I just want you to believe that I have no intention of letting anyone know where you are. If your secret leaks out, it won't be because of me. Someone else from Bryant Lake may pick up a copy of the tabloid somewhere and see through your so-called disguise."

"I suppose that could happen," he conceded.

"Okay, if any reporters come banging on your door just remember that, will you?"

"I'll try," Paul said softly. He'd released her arm, but he was still standing very close to her. He was also blocking the route from where she stood to the front door. She saw that he'd either have to move or she'd have to edge around him if she were to get by.

She said, "That's all," and started to edge around him.

"Wait a minute," Paul commanded, and Pam stopped still, even though this time he didn't reach out to detain her. "Is that the only reason you came over here? Because you couldn't get to sleep unless you were sure I believed you wouldn't turn me in?"

All right, her rationale sounded silly, the way he put it. Pam's cheeks flamed again.

Paul's voice softened, and there was something close to tenderness in the way he looked at her. "You know," he said, "if I were around you very much you might actually restore a lot of faith I thought had gone down the tube." He added wryly, "Lousy pun not intended."

The tenderness was still there as he reached out one of his wonderful hands and rubbed his thumb along Pam's jawline. Then, as if this were a scene being filmed in slow motion, he cupped her chin, fanning his fingers out and moving them back and forth gently. "You're quite a person, Pamela Martin," he told her, his low voice mesmerizing. "You're different, very different I'd say, and I like that. You really do have your own kind of ethics, don't you?"

His touch was driving Pam crazy. It was all she could do to stand still. She wanted to fling herself into his arms, plunge her hands into his thick dark hair, pillow her head against his broad chest, revel in the hard male tautness of his body.

Again—did she think she was Angela Santoro?

What had he said? Oh, that she had her own kind of ethics. Pam tried to find her voice so that she could tell him that long ago her father had instilled a code of ethics in her—where both journalism and life were concerned—that she could never possibly forget. But her voice had gone somewhere else.

Paul murmured, "It would be easy to believe in you."

He switched off the light switch he'd turned on a few minutes ago. Lit only by the glow from a corner lamp, the atmosphere in the room immediately turned intimate. The music, low and soft, was a mood enhancer.... Not, Pam thought, that she needed one.

Paul gently tugged her toward him. His arms went around her. Pam stumbled into his embrace and for a moment knew a sense of sanctuary. But then she plunged into a bottomless sea of emotions that rocked her.

This man who was holding her—by whatever name he might be called—was setting her afire. His lips touched hers, brushing lightly, at first, as if they were testing unknown territory. Then they lingered, pressed, moved in a wordless language more eloquent than speech. His tongue teased her mouth, urging her to let him invade this first of her secret regions. Pam responded, involuntarily clutching his shoulders as their kiss deepened.

Slowly Paul trailed his fingers down her back. Then he sculpted her waist and gently prodded the edges of her shirt until he was caressing the warmth of her flesh, then molding the smooth roundness of her breasts with his palms.

Pam discovered that time *could* stop, suspending people in a magical crystal sphere where there was only feeling. She yielded to this incredible rapture that was flowing through her, sweet and hot, an invasion that she wanted to go on forever. And when Paul suddenly stopped, his hands all at once still and rigid, the shock was profound.

He withdrew from her so suddenly that Pam literally went off balance. She actually staggered, and as he steadied her, she felt him shudder and heard his ragged sigh.

"I think we'd better put on the brakes," he muttered.

The letdown was traumatic.

Pam tried to tell herself that he was right...of course. She supposed she should be grateful for his restraint, for his consideration of her. But she wasn't.

She trekked back to her house alone. Paul had offered to accompany her. Pam had insisted that she'd be perfectly safe making this small safari by herself.

She'd needed to get away from him. She couldn't help feeling a sense of rejection, even though she knew it would have been madness to continue along the kind of course they'd started on. But she wondered if madness might not be preferable to sanity.

Paul had looked very solemn as he'd said good-night to her. Pam, gazing through her bedroom window at the stars that always seemed so bright here in the north country, wondered if from now on he'd take real pains to avoid her.

He didn't.

She was making coffee the next morning when Paul— having approached her cottage via the lakefront— clumped up the porch steps and appeared at her kitchen door.

"I've been jogging," he explained. "Decided it would be a good idea to start getting a little morning exercise." He added, "I saw your kitchen light on."

"I almost always get up early." Pam was trying not to react visibly to the sight of him in shorts and a thick, green wool sweater. "I just made bacon and eggs," she went on. "Interested?"

"Definitely." To her surprise, he grinned.

He polished off bacon, eggs, toast and three cups of coffee without saying much, then asked, "Got anything special planned for today?"

Pam thought about her father's journal, which—she reminded herself—was her number one priority. She'd been intending to get started on her project today. But...

"No, I don't have anything special planned," she said, too curious about what Paul might have on his mind to give him any other answer.

"I thought it might be interesting to wander around a little," he ventured. "Maybe head up toward Quebec. The border's not far from here."

"No." A thought struck Pam. "Probably we wouldn't be asked for any identification crossing the border, but one can never be sure. Do you want to risk that?"

He shrugged. "No problem. My driver's license is in my real name. I even have my glasses on in the picture. The Trooper's registered in my real name."

"Sounds all right," Pam agreed.

They set out half an hour later. The foliage was beginning to change, and the day was perfect. Pam soon realized that she was viewing everything from a purely euphoric viewpoint, and she warned herself that she mustn't get carried away by the man at her side.

They chose the back roads for the most part, where there was so little traffic this time of year they could loiter as much as they wanted to.

She'd been afraid that she'd be ill at ease with Paul, after last night's sizzling episode. But, as the miles clicked by, she was surprised at how comfortable she felt—especially when he was simply being himself. He seemed so relaxed.

Evidently he'd decided he could trust her—or was willing to take a chance.

Paul adroitly led Pam into talking about herself, and she found herself telling him about her father and the especially important role he'd played in her life.

She talked about the wonderful times she and her father had spent at Bryant Lake, recounted the way they'd often rowed out to the middle of the lake and fished, early in the morning.

"There are bass and perch and some landlocked salmon," she reported.

"You need a freshwater license, don't you?" Paul asked.

"Yes."

"Got one?"

"No. But you can get licenses at Cullum's store."

"Let's," he suggested, and she nodded agreement.

Pam, lulled by their easy mood, was startled when he suddenly said, "Yesterday you were talking about having a lot of decisions to make."

Pam's eyebrows rose. "You have quite a memory."

"Comes from having to memorize lines on a daily basis." He waited, then persisted. "*Are* you thinking about getting married?"

Pam considered that, and said honestly, "I don't know."

It was Paul's turn to raise a quizzical eyebrow. "You don't know?"

"There's a man in Boston," she admitted.

"Oh?"

"I don't know if I love him," Pam blurted, then caught her breath. That was a sentiment about Alfred she'd never voiced so succinctly even to herself.

Paul negotiated a curve, then observed, "If you don't know that you love him, why are you even thinking about marrying him?"

"Hmm . . . I suppose because I want to get married and have kids."

"Not good enough. I'd like to get married and have kids, too. But I long ago decided that I probably never will."

"Why not?"

He shrugged. "I'd expect too much from a woman."

"What do you mean?"

"I'd expect her to love me as much as I'd need to love her, if I ever seriously got to the marrying stage. I mean . . . love *me*. Not what I may look like or what I seem to be."

"You're thinking of Griffith McQueen, M.D. again."

"Unfortunately, I never can forget him for very long. I think my biggest fear is that even if I manage to see him dead and buried he'll still rise to haunt me."

"His isn't the only part you've ever played, is it?"

"I had minor parts in a couple of other soaps first."

"Well . . . once Griffith McQueen, M.D. is dead, you can go on to other roles, can't you?"

"I'm identified so closely with him I'm afraid it may be beyond my capability to create an entirely new image," Paul confessed. "I told you I don't have that much talent."

"I find that hard to believe."

"I should take one of the jobs on Broadway that are offered to me from time to time, then maybe you'd find it easier to believe. On TV, we work on a day-to-day basis. The actors are handed a new script each morning. We go over our parts and memorize them, we have one rehearsal and then we shoot. In order to keep within the budget it's important to do your damnedest to get it right the first time.

"For me, anyway, the daily stint becomes a matter of rote," Paul said. "I learn my lines, I speak them. Because I'm not a good actor, I pay a lot of attention to the stage business. Watch an episode, and you'll see that I do a lot of fooling around with a scalpel, for instance, or I concentrate on the appointment pad on my desk, or I pay a lot of attention to scrubbing up before I go into the OR. In regard to that—I know some actors who've played physician parts so intensely they've just about become convinced they actually are doctors. I suppose my medical knowledge has been augmented, thanks to Griffith, but believe me, I'm not about to put out my shingle and book office hours."

Pam laughed.

"Anyway," Paul went on, "if you consider the segments on an average soap, one person isn't on screen *that* long, so it doesn't take a genius to get the lines down pat. It becomes something you just *do*, sort of like brushing your teeth." He halted. "Whatever got me into this? Let's talk about something else."

"Let's not," Pam contradicted. "Hearing about your work is really interesting." That certainly was true, but she also had a strong feeling that Paul needed to talk about his work with someone objective right now, needed to get a lot of the things about his job off his chest.

His job? It seemed odd to put such an ordinary tag on something so glamorous.

"How did you become Griffith McQueen?" she asked him.

"How did I *become* Griffith?" He looked amused. "Well, I guess we can blame Jerry Bernstein for that. He's the one who discovered me."

"In Nebraska?"

"Nebraska?"

"I've read that you were discovered working as a bartender at a popular night spot in Omaha. You'd been brought up in Nebraska on a farm your father owned."

"Hype," Paul informed her. "Jerry invented that story. I've never even been to Nebraska. Jerry merely liked the Midwest image. Thought it seemed very healthy and American. Actually, I'm from Georgia, as I will always remember only too well. Not that I have anything against Georgia—and it, too, is ultimately American—but I had a helluva time getting rid of my Southern accent."

"Why did Jerry switch the locale?"

"Mainly to draw attention away from the fact that my origins left a lot to be desired, from a publicity point of view," Paul said grimly. He hesitated, gave her a long look, then admitted, "My father not only didn't own a farm, I never had a father."

Pam stared at him, shocked.

"I was born in a small city in western Georgia that's not far from a large army base," he said. "My mother was a local girl. My father was in the military. My mother became pregnant. My father, at the most opportune of moments, was transferred. He took off, and she never saw him again.

"I went to school, there in Columbus," he continued. "After a time, my mother married. I hated my stepfather, and he hated me. Anyway, my mother and her husband eventually had three other kids, so they didn't have the time or energy to bother much with me, or to raise too big a fuss when I ran away. That was halfway through my junior year in high school. I'd intended to stay home until I finished school, but the time came when I couldn't take the constant hassle and haranguing any longer. I went to Washington and worked at all kinds of essentially mindless jobs and went to school nights until finally I got my high school diploma.

"I was waiting tables in a Georgetown restaurant when I met Jerry Bernstein."

"And he steered you toward television acting?"

"Yeah...and sometimes I'm not sure I thank him for it. Certainly I've made more money than I possibly could have any other way. And I have to admit that being a celebrity does have its highs, though most of the time I hate that kind of notoriety, which is pretty much what celebrity fame amounts to. But there are times when I wonder what I might have done with my life if Jerry had never chosen to have dinner at Les Trois Étoiles that night."

He slanted a smile toward Pam. "Too late to speculate about that."

"Maybe, but...what did Jerry Bernstein do? Just take one look at you and..."

"Essentially, that's just about what he did," Paul admitted. "Jerry has an eye for so-called photogenic faces. He watched me, and Jerry says that when something really hits him, a little buzzer goes off inside his head. He insists that day the buzzer nearly drove him crazy.

"Jerry can be one of the world's most persuasive individuals. That's why he's so good at his job. He convinced me I should move to New York, he staked me to the money needed to put together a glossy photo portfolio and then he landed me half a dozen TV jobs doing commercials. With those under my belt, Jerry moved on and got me the minor soap parts. Then came the moment when they were auditioning for the Griffith McQueen, M.D. role in *When Tomorrow Comes,* which was scheduled to start production that fall, and Jerry pushed me into trying for the part.

"I can remember walking into the studio and thinking, 'This is insane. I'm not even an actor.' Next thing I knew, I had the part. Now Griffith McQueen has taken over my life and . . .

"Enough," he said firmly. "Anyway, I'm hungry. How about you?"

Pam had never known a person who could switch subjects so abruptly, yet with such adroitness. But, as a matter of fact she *was* hungry.

"Yes," she admitted, wishing that he hadn't chosen to cut off his story at that particular point. She especially wanted to know more about Angela Santoro.

High on a hillside they discovered an inn that was still open. The dining room windows looked out over a babbling brook. Beyond, in a pasture, cows grazed contentedly. In the distance the Green Mountains smudged the sky.

Perfection, Pam thought. Savor it. Hoard it. Enjoy each minute you spend with him because nothing like this can last forever.

They feasted on cheese and bacon quiche, they talked, though not about anything personal. Later, they drove almost to the Canadian border but decided to

leave their exploration of Quebec's environs for another day. On the way home they stopped at a farm and
bought maple syrup and apples.

Though Pam had enjoyed similar outings with her
father in past years, this day with Paul was filled with
entirely new experiences. She had not fully appreciated
that there could be so much pleasure in sharing even the
simplest things with the right person.

By the time Paul pulled up in front of Pam's cottage
she was afraid—terribly afraid—that she'd fallen in
love.

Chapter Five

Pam pushed down the handle, opened the car door, then turned toward Paul. "Thanks for today," she said, ready to exit as soon as she'd made this small speech. Her emotions were in a turmoil. She needed a little private time to straighten herself out.

To her surprise, he asked, "Aren't you going to invite me in?"

During the last part of their drive home, Paul had been silent. Pam had thought perhaps he was tired of her company. But now he added, "If I remember right, there was a fair bit of that wine left after lunch the other day. Unless you finished it in the meantime."

"I didn't finish it." Her hesitation was brief. "Come on in."

They took the wine out on the porch and settled down in the blue rockers. The sun had slipped behind the mountains, illuminating the horizon and leaving an iridescent sheen on the water. Overhead, a flock of honking Canada geese flew by, and Pam said, "Fall. The wild geese always make me think of fall."

"You sound as though the idea of fall makes you sad."

"It does, in a way. Oh, I love autumn in New England. Who wouldn't? But then the holidays begin and . . ."

"Holidays mean loneliness?"

"Yes . . . I suppose you could say that."

"I know." He nodded. "Sometimes you can be in a crowd and still be lonely. Often, I have that feeling—"

Inside the house, the telephone pealed.

Pam froze. This was the first time the phone had rung since she'd been at Bryant Lake. Linda Bailey was the only one she had given the phone number to, just before she left Boston. Could Linda have become so pressured by Alfred that she'd violated a confidence?

Pam couldn't imagine Linda betraying her like that. On the other hand, Linda's job might be on the line, though that seemed pretty farfetched. Alfred could be both insistent and persistent, but she doubted he'd fire someone for sticking up for a friend.

"Aren't you going to answer the phone?" Paul asked.

Pam got up reluctantly. "Yes, I suppose I'd better."

She hoped the caller would hang up before she crossed the living room. That didn't happen, but Pam was relieved to hear that it was Linda rather than Alfred at the other end of the line.

Linda said immediately, "I know you asked me not to call unless it was critical, but in my opinion this is critical. I have to talk to you, Pam. Alfred's driving me up a wall. I'll go crazy if you don't contact him. He

knows very damned well I know where you are. I've
never had a poker face. I only wish I did."

"Let me call you back," Pam urged.

"Let's deal with this now."

"I can't talk to you now." Pam was aware that Paul
had moved off the porch and was standing in the living
room doorway. "I'll call you later."

"I'm going out." Linda's voice was icy.

"Okay, when can I reach you?"

"I should be back by midnight." Linda slammed
down the receiver.

Pam stared at the handset. Telephones could be a
blessing—but there were times when they could also be
a curse. She'd made a mistake in giving Linda her
number. She shouldn't even have given Linda her address at the lake. She'd put a good friend in a very difficult spot. But it had seemed important that one person
in the entire world know where she was.

Paul asked, "Why wouldn't you talk now?"

Pam turned on him. "I don't care much for people
who eavesdrop."

"Sorry about that. I'll ask again. Why couldn't you
talk now?"

"I don't think that's any of your business."

"I'd like to be sure of that."

Pam heard the suspicion in his voice, and her control broke. "You may think headline stories about you
are the most important things in the world, but that
doesn't mean I agree," she stormed. "Matter of fact, I
wouldn't write a story about you if I got the biggest bo-
nus in newspaper history for doing it. You don't need
any more ego trips. As it is, I wonder if there's a big
enough mirror in the universe to reflect your head."

Pam couldn't believe the sound she heard.

Paul was laughing.

He laughed so hard he finally dug a handkerchief out of his pocket, took off his glasses and wiped his eyes.

"That's marvelous." He chuckled. "You're wonderful, Pam."

Without the glasses on, Pam got the full effect of the silvery eyes that were one of Griffith McQueen, M.D.'s trademarks. To her chagrin she discovered she was not immune to their effect, no matter how angry she was with Paul.

She also discovered that without time to retrench, her treacherous emotions were sliding over the edge. Tears filled her eyes and spilled down her cheeks.

Paul saw the tears and protested. "Hey, I'm sorry. I should have realized that call upset you."

He came to her, held out his arms, and Pam went into them. She let him hold her close while she pillowed her head against his shoulder and sobbed. She hadn't realized how tense she'd been for a long, long time until her tears flowed, dampening the green wool of Paul's sweater until he wore a large, wet patch.

After a time, he tugged her down to the couch. He still kept his arm around her as, finally, she began to quiet down. He'd given her his handkerchief. Now she dabbed at her eyes and, thoroughly annoyed with herself, said, "I'm sorry." She touched his sweater. "You're wet."

He smiled. "That's okay. I'll dry."

She snuggled against him, unable to push away from the comfort he was offering. He waited awhile, then asked gently, "Want to talk about it?"

"Yes," she decided.

She drew in a deep breath, then let the air out slowly. "That was my best friend on the phone. Her name's Linda Bailey. She was calling from Boston."

"It didn't sound like you were having a very fulfilling conversation," Paul observed mildly.

"I knew what Linda was calling about and I didn't want to get into it."

"Want to tell me what she was calling about?"

"Alfred."

"The guy who wants to marry you?"

Pam pulled back to look at him. "How did you make that connection?"

"Need you ask?"

Pam didn't know what to say.

"As I get the picture, Alfred wants to marry you but you don't know whether you love him or not."

"You're making it sound like a soap-opera plot."

"Subplot," Paul corrected.

She darted a disapproving glance at him and he said swiftly, "I'm not making fun. I'd say this is pretty serious if you're even remotely thinking about marrying Alfred when you're not sure you love him. Why would you want to marry someone unless you didn't think you could live without them?"

Pam said, "Alfred would...make a good husband. He's in his early forties, he's co-owner and president of a Boston public relations and advertising agency, he's never been married and he's at a time in his life when he really wants a wife and a family. He's attractive, we come from similar backgrounds, we have a lot in common."

"Doesn't sound like enough," Paul said.

"Enough for what?"

"Enough to compensate for not loving him. Hell, if you loved the guy you wouldn't have to torture yourself trying to figure out whether or not you wanted to share the rest of your life with him."

"You sound so sure of yourself."

"I'm only sure of the way I believe someone should feel if they're seriously thinking of marriage," Paul told her.

The last remnants of daylight were fading outside. Night was taking over from dusk, and it was dark in the living room. But Pam made no move to turn on a light. There was a deepened sense of sharing to sitting here in the dark with Paul, his arm wrapped around her shoulder.

She rested her head back on that shoulder, which still wasn't dry. Paul nuzzled her forehead, brushing his lips across her hairline. Thoughts about Alfred fled. She was too conscious of the man at her side to think of anyone else.

Then Paul straightened, and it was he who reached out to switch on the nearby table lamp. He said, "I'd better give you the chance to call your friend back."

Releasing Pam, Paul rose. "Just don't make any quick decisions." His voice was husky.

Last night he'd told her they'd better put on the brakes. Though those words were not rephrased, they could as well have been spoken again.

Pam wished he didn't have quite so much good sense, so much restraint. Because she had a very strong feeling that right now he was feeling just about the way she was.

Pam was tempted to tell Paul she couldn't call Linda back till midnight, but she didn't. Instead, she loaned him her flashlight for his walk home.

Once Paul had left, Pam trailed out to the porch and reclaimed the wine bottle and their two glasses. She was determined to keep her promise and call Linda at midnight. After a time, she thought about making a sandwich but she wasn't hungry. Still later, she brewed some coffee, hoping it would keep her awake, because she was getting sleepier and sleepier.

She settled down with an exciting mystery, trusting that it would be such a page-turner she couldn't close her eyes. But her lids were very heavy, and she dozed.

As if by fate, she awakened at three minutes to midnight. She dialed Linda's number, but there was no answer.

Pam settled down again, and read for the next half hour. Then she dialed Linda's number again, but the phone just rang and rang.

Was Linda so irked she deliberately was not answering the phone? Or did she really have such an interesting date she hadn't gotten home yet?

Once again, Pam picked up her book. But this time when she fell asleep she stayed asleep.

Dawn's gray fingers were creeping across the living room when Pam woke up. She stood, stretched and groaned. She'd been curled up on the couch, and now she felt like a human pretzel. Her sleep had been restless, dream-plagued. She felt hung over.

She started for the shower, then had a better idea. The lake water would be frigid so early in the morning. What could be a better eye-opener than a good workout swim?

Pam slipped on a swimsuit, headed for the lakefront and tested the water with her big toe. She was prepared for the shock but she still drew back and gasped. The water temperature was geared to polar bears.

She was tempted to retreat and settle for the hot shower after all, but... that would be quitting. Right now she needed a challenge, and also the zest that meeting the challenge would give her.

She lost no time wading out to a point where she could plunge in, then she struck out, cleaving through the water with strong, even strokes. By habit, she headed toward the middle of the lake, then turned left.

As she swam, she kept expecting to warm up a little. She put extra exertion into her strokes, swimming harder and faster than usual. But she still felt as though someone had turned on a cold-water tap inside her veins.

Then, in a second she'd never forget, her left thigh was gripped by a cramp so strong it took instant control of her body. The pain was so excruciating she called out, and her mouth at once filled up with water. She spit as she tried to work out the cramp, struggling against an agony so intense that she'd have no chance of getting through this unless the cramp went away as swiftly as it had come.

The pain was clutching her calf as well as her thigh, and she thrashed wildly. She grabbed her leg with both hands, trying desperately to massage the contorted muscles, but that proved to be impossible. It was as if a giant octopus had its tentacles around her and was twisting tighter and tighter....

Then she went under.

Pam sank beneath the lake's surface, and the icy water filled her ears, her nostrils. She tried to keep her mouth shut but it was a superhuman effort, because age-old instinct made it almost impossible not to cry out. She rose to the surface, flailing her arms, trying to tilt her face up to the sky, trying to scream, though she knew how high the odds were against anyone hearing her. Then she sank again. And in her last moment of consciousness before she was enveloped by icy blankets, Pam knew that life was ebbing out of her and she was drifting toward oblivion.

Pam imagined she heard someone calling her name. At the same time, she felt a weight pressing against her chest. Pressing again and again.

She opened her eyes, and her vision blurred. But through the hazy mist she could see Paul bent over her. And she knew it was his hands pushing at her chest in a steady, even rhythm, pushing over and over again.

As she began to see more clearly, she realized he was soaking wet. Water streamed from his dark hair and wet his cheeks. She looked more closely. Some of the water was coming out of his eyes.

She tried to speak. But she could only squawk something unintelligible.

It was enough. Paul sat back on his haunches and stared at her, his hands still poised over her breasts.

"Oh, God," he said, his voice almost as hoarse as hers.

Pam tried to speak again, but instead she retched. She managed to turn her head to one side, but nothing came out. She had not even had coffee this morning. There was nothing to throw up.

She felt Paul's hand on her forehead. His skin was warm, and—oddly—the warmth made her shiver. She was ice-cold all the way through.

Paul stood, and she saw he was wearing soggy blue cotton briefs. He leaned over and scooped her up in his arms. Pam, tight in his embrace, blacked out again.

This time, when consciousness filtered back, Pam was in Paul's bed. She discovered she was wearing a thick terry robe, and he'd covered her with both a blanket and a quilt. But she was still freezing.

As if on cue, he appeared, carrying a mug from which steam was escaping.

"Coffee," he said. "It's very hot, but try to drink some."

Pam tried. The coffee nearly scalded her throat, but the burning sensation actually felt wonderful. But then she murmured, "I'm...sorry. I'm afraid if I drink any more I won't be able to keep it down."

By the time she finished speaking, her teeth were chattering.

Paul touched her arm and scowled. "You're like ice." With a swift gesture, he turned back the blanket and the quilt and slid into bed alongside her.

He took her in his arms and pulled her against him. Chills rocked her body, but then gradually they began to subside as she drew on his warmth. Paul held her very close, and Pam thought, before she fell asleep, that never in her life had she known such tenderness.

When she awoke again, she was warm...but the place at her side was empty, and she felt an incredible sense of loss. She also was disoriented. Paul had drawn the shades in the room; she had no idea what time it was.

She sat up and swung her legs over the side of the bed. At first she felt giddy, but gradually she steadied. Finally, she tested out her strength by standing. Then by walking carefully, one foot placed slowly in front of the other as she moved across the room. She was shaky...but alive.

She used the bathroom, then peered at herself in the mirror over the sink. She looked terrible. Her hair was still damp, hanging limp around her shoulders. She was ghostly pale, and her eyes seemed enormous.

She shuddered, remembering the icy water closing in over her. By some miracle, Paul had found her.

She owed him her life.

She padded back into the bedroom just as he appeared in the opposite doorway. She had the odd feeling that right now they were operating on an identical channel. For this time, at least, he was a part of her and she a part of him. They were tuned into each other.

"You shouldn't have gotten up," he said. "Not without calling for help."

"I'm all right."

"The hell you are." He smiled slightly. "You should see yourself."

"I just did."

Paul's eyes lingered on her face, and she couldn't read their expression. But then he said huskily, "For a while, I thought I'd lost you."

Again, he switched subjects abruptly. "Climb back into bed and hang in," he instructed. "I'm going to get you something to eat."

He was gone before Pam could protest. She had to laugh at herself as she climbed into bed like an obedient child. She nestled against Paul's pillows, appreciating their comfort, appreciating just being warm, appreciating more than anything else being *alive*.

Paul came back with a tray on which he'd put a bowl of soup and a plate of crackers. The soup was delicious, and Pam discovered she actually was hungry.

She paused to say, "This is so good I can't believe it came out of a can."

"It didn't."

"Where did you get it?"

"I made it." Paul laughed at her expression. "You didn't believe me when I told you I was going to make you a Greek dinner, I guess. I like to cook. Problem is, when I do it I overdo it. So usually I stick to something like soup and freeze most of what I make."

He waited till she'd finished, then picked up the tray. "Now," he instructed, "you go back to sleep for a while."

"I've slept for hours."

"Close those beautiful blue eyes of yours and you'll sleep for more hours," he predicted. "Which is what you should be doing. Sleep's the best possible therapy after an ordeal like you've had."

Paul had put on chinos and a red knit shirt. He'd shaved and carefully combed his hair. But despite the immaculate appearance, his face was shadowed by fatigue, and he looked as though he'd been through quite an ordeal himself.

Pam said, "I . . . I can't believe what happened. You must have come out after me."

He was silent.

"That's what happened, isn't it?" she persisted. "You rescued me."

"Yes."

"How could you have known I was out in the middle of the lake with a cramp in my leg?"

"I didn't." Paul gripped the tray he was holding a little tighter. "I didn't sleep very well last night. I was . . . restless. This morning when daylight came I decided one way to clear my head would be to go for a run along the lake. I was just coming out of the house when I saw you wading into the water. I was tempted to put on a swimsuit and join you, but frankly, running appealed to me more than plunging into that ice water. So,

I jogged along the shoreline in the same direction you were swimming and..."

Paul shook his head. "I don't even want to talk about it."

"I have to know," Pam insisted.

"Well...when you turned, I turned, too. My idea was to intercept you once you got out of the water and ask you to come to my place for breakfast this time. Then...you stopped swimming and I saw you start to thrash and I knew you were in trouble. I stripped off my clothes and went in after you. I was scared to hell and gone that you'd go down before I got to you and I wouldn't be able to find you. You..."

"Go on."

"You did go down. But I dived and...and I managed to clutch your hair. Then I got you to shore and started CPR on you. I wanted to go for help but there was no way I could leave you, not even to get as far as your phone. It never struck me before how isolated it is around here this time of year.

"When you opened your eyes," Paul said, "I felt I'd witnessed a miracle."

Pam didn't speak. She couldn't.

Paul urged gently, "Go to sleep."

Pam nodded. He was in the doorway before she found her voice and called his name.

He turned. "You saved my life," she told him.

Paul shook his head, a mix of emotions playing over his face.

"Yes," she repeated, "you saved my life." She managed to smile at him. "I owe you one, Paul Martin."

Paul's return smile was tired, lopsided. "I'll remember that," he told her.

Chapter Six

It was hours later when Pam woke up again. Soft music wafted in from the living room. This time, Paul was playing a mix of fifties favorites. Pam lay back for a few minutes and listened, letting the melodies mellow and soothe her. Then she went to find Paul.

He was ensconced in one of the chintzy armchairs, reading a book whose title she couldn't glimpse. As he got to his feet, he looked Pam over from head to foot. "How are you doing?" His concern warmed her.

"Matter of fact, I feel pretty good," she told him. She paused. "Paul, thank you for everything."

That sounded so inadequate.

"Are you thinking of leaving?" Paul queried. "That comes on like a farewell line."

"I need to go home and put some clothes on." Pam was suddenly very conscious of the fact that, under his terry robe, she was as naked as a newborn.

"Tell me what you want and I'll get it for you," he offered.

"I don't know what I want. It might help if I knew what time it is," she amended. "I mean...then I'd have a better idea of how I should dress."

"Formal or informal?" he teased. Then added gently, "I don't think you should be alone tonight, Pam. Why don't you stay here?"

She peered out the window. "It's dark out. How late is it?"

"Nearly nine."

"I slept through an entire day?"

"Yes."

He didn't need to add that she'd very nearly fallen into a kind of sleep that could have lasted forever. She knew that, and she shivered.

Right now, she felt so helpless. She was discovering she couldn't think clearly, she couldn't express herself fully. She wanted to let Paul know—really know—how grateful she was to him, how indebted. But the right words wouldn't come.

It occurred to her maybe he didn't want either her gratitude or her indebtedness.

Nearly drowning wasn't any help toward gaining emotional stability, Pam thought wryly. She was tense and jittery.

"Come out to the kitchen," Paul invited. "I'll make you some supper."

"I just ate."

"You had that soup hours ago."

"Time's...confused," Pam confessed.

"I know. Look, sweetheart, I'm going to tuck you in again. Then I bet if I bring you some hot cocoa you'll go right to sleep and you'll sleep till morning. That's what you need.''

There was only one bedroom in the cottage, and it contained one double bed. Earlier, that hadn't mattered. Earlier, in fact, Paul had shared that bed with Pam—but she reminded herself that he'd done that for therapeutic reasons.

Now she had recovered physically but she had other concerns. Everything she was feeling seemed more intense than usual, sharpened by a heightened perception. The kind of perception, she'd heard, that comes to people who've narrowly escaped death.

Shaken, she knew she couldn't stay here in Paul's house tonight. Even if he gave her his bed and slept on the living room couch, they'd be too close to each other. She had leaned on his strength today, literally warmed herself with his body heat. Much more of that kind of thing and she'd slip into a dependency on him that wouldn't be easy to rid herself of.

He had saved her life, but that didn't mean he was responsible for her.

Paul said, ''Pam, will you sit down before you fall down. You're swaying back and forth.''

He was right. Pam had to admit she *was* swaying. She was weaker than she'd thought, and she plopped down on the nearest chair.

''Damn,'' Paul muttered. ''You need to see a doctor.''

''No,'' Pam protested, ''I don't. Really I don't. I'm fine.''

''I'm not sure. You were so cold. I'd never forgive myself if you had some serious repercussions from this.''

"I won't have any serious repercussions." Except where you're concerned, Pam thought. After sharing today with you, how can I go back to the way I was before this happened?

Paul was frowning. "I know you're strong, healthy. But you're human, sweetheart. By tomorrow, if you're not one hundred percent I'm going to ask Bert Cullum to recommend the best doctor around."

She closed her eyes briefly. That was the second time he'd called her sweetheart.

He decided, "For now, I guess I should take you back to your place. You'll be more comfortable there."

Before Pam knew what he was about to do, he leaned over the chair and picked her up in his arms.

"Wait a minute!" she protested. "You can't carry me all the way to my house."

"Don't bet on that. However, I plan only to take you out to the Trooper. We'll drive to your house, all right?" He was striding toward the door as he spoke.

When they reached her cottage, Paul insisted that Pam stay in the car while he went in to switch on some lights and her electric blanket. But before he could come back out to get her, she traipsed down to the cottage herself.

She heard water running as soon as she walked in. He was fixing a hot bath for her.

She smiled. The man did think of everything.

After her bath, Pam found Paul in her kitchen making toast and omelets for both of them. Though she still wasn't hungry, she wouldn't have dared refuse the plate of food he set in front of her.

Later, she quickly learned there was no way she could persuade him to leave her alone tonight.

"I'll sleep in the living room," he said. And that was that.

Her need for some space from him hadn't lessened. But, Pam had to admit, she was in no shape to do much about anything tonight. Some basic physical demands that had nothing to do with sensual chemistry took over. She was still suffering from the effects of today's ordeal. Nature relentlessly took its course, and nature's prescription was for more sleep.

When she awoke the next morning, the house was very still. So still that Pam thought Paul must have left. But when she pattered out to the living room she found him on her couch, which obviously had been most inadequate. His legs were so long they dangled over the armrest. His head, propped on a couple of small, square pillows, was tilted at what looked like a very uncomfortable angle.

She made no sound, but he nevertheless became aware of her presence before she'd been standing at his side for more than a few seconds. He opened his eyes and smiled a slow, easy smile that melted Pam's heart.

"Hey," he said, "am I dreaming—or are you for real? You look like an angel."

Pam had brushed her tangled hair and, as she splashed cold water on her face, noted that she still looked pale and—she thought—haggard. She was wearing a pale blue granny gown. She couldn't imagine that she looked in the least angelic, and she laughed.

"I guess you really do need glasses," she told him.

He reached out a hand. Pam took it and let him tug her to his side. He said, "You look great fuzzy, and you look great sharp. Do you know how beautiful you are?"

"No," Pam said honestly.

Paul's smile deepened. "You're slightly lovelier than lovely."

She shook her head reprovingly. "What a tease you are!"

She was thinking of the beautiful women he worked with—like Angela Santoro. She couldn't hold a candle to any of them.

"I'm not teasing," he insisted. "I'm serious. You're a natural beauty, Pam. You don't need a lot of artifice to get you ready to face the world. What you have goes way beyond physical beauty. That's God-given. People don't have much choice about their looks, after all. But I think they do have control over character. You are very special."

He chuckled. "If I keep on," he said, "there may not be a 'big enough mirror in the universe to reflect your head.'"

Pam flushed as he quoted her. She started to pull away, but he kept a grip on her hand.

"I—I should never have said that to you," she stammered, evading the amused gleam in his silvery eyes. "To tell the truth, you seem to have very little vanity, and I have to admit I thought all actors must be pretty vain."

"What did you say about people being different and our respecting their individuality?"

"Is every word I speak to you going to come back to haunt me?"

"Maybe."

Paul pulled her toward him as he spoke. Then he cupped the back of her head with his hands and drew her even closer until her face was only inches from his. It was she who closed in the distance, her lips seeking his.

She wouldn't have believed that just a kiss could do this to someone—send spirals of delight through a person's body, twisting like rainbow-colored satin streamers. Pam yielded to the bright beauty of feelings that were clear and intense, for there was nothing to cloud them. She let herself go with the natural rhythm of her instinct. She and Paul clung and caressed and then simply held on to each other—and for right now that was enough.

They were still clinging when they heard the clatter of wheels on gravel. Paul said, "Sounds like someone's stopped out front."

Their magic spell was broken as he released Pam, stood and went to the living room window. "The mail truck," Paul said. "Early in the day for him to come, isn't it?"

"Yes, it is."

"The mailman's getting out, but he isn't going to the box. Hell, he's coming *here*."

Pam said quickly, "I'll see what he wants."

She opened the front door and forced a smile as she greeted the mailman. "Hello, Mr. Beeman."

Henry Beeman was a small, thin man with a shock of white hair. He'd been white-haired ever since Pam could remember.

"Morning," he greeted. "Got an Express Mail letter for you."

The letter, she saw, was addressed to P. Martin, and was from Jerry Bernstein. It occurred to her that this was not the time to straighten out the mail mix-up.

She signed for the letter, then murmured, "Thanks a lot," and watched the mailman retreat before she walked across the room and handed the envelope to Paul.

He glanced at it and muttered, "What now?" as he ripped it open.

Pam knew from his expression that he didn't like what he was reading.

That was confirmed when he scowled and said sourly, "This is just what I need."

"What's happened?"

"Angela has decided something terrible must have happened to me and she's going to hire a team of top-notch private detectives to track me down."

"You think they could find you?"

"I don't know. Frankly, I doubt it... but how can I be sure?" He ran an agitated hand through his hair. "God! All I'm asking is to be let alone. I don't know why Jerry can't come out and make the flat statement that I have absolutely no intention of going back on the show. But I intend to call him and find out."

He glanced at the clock on the mantel. "It's not even nine. Too early to get hold of Jerry. He never gets into his office before ten. Suppose I make us a pot of coffee? Personally I could use a caffeine fix."

"I'll make the coffee." Pam led the way to her kitchen.

Paul paced the floor restlessly, even after she'd handed him a mug of hot coffee. She watched him stop at the window, stare out at the lake, then turn away and start pacing again.

"I know how you're feeling," she said at last.

He swung toward her. "You do?"

She nodded. "Trapped. That's the way you feel, isn't it?"

"Yes."

"Paul? How can I put this to you? Even though you may feel trapped, don't burn your bridges." She smiled. "How clichéd can one get?"

He said soberly, "I can't think of any bridges I want to remain standing, Pam."

"Don't be so sure. You've worked very hard to get where you are."

"I fell into a pot of luck," he said, scoffing.

"I don't think you give yourself enough credit." She was serious about that. "You act as though anyone could create a character like Griffith McQueen, M.D."

"I didn't create Griffith, love. Three writers scrambled their brains thinking him up, and since they caved in to their ulcers, several more have worked on the scripts."

"Paul..."

He'd begun pacing again. He stopped.

"I don't think you're as jaundiced as you appear to be," Pam said.

He'd put on his glasses. The lenses glittered as he faced her. "Oh, really? What makes you say that?"

"From everything I've read or heard about being in the limelight, once a person has had that kind of attention it isn't easy to give it up."

"I can't wait to give it up."

"You think so. But you'll miss the applause."

"What applause? I've never heard any applause—not when I'm working, anyway. We don't have a studio audience."

"You know what I mean."

"I'm afraid I do. You evidently feel my ego needs continual feeding."

She sighed. "Is that so strange? You're not just...any old person, Paul."

"I can't believe you're saying that. Just what or who is 'any old person'? Give me a definition."

"You know what I mean," Pam said again.

Paul frowned. "You keep telling me that, and the problem is I think I do know what you mean. You think I've cast myself in the role of a kid playing hooky, and once the kick is gone I'll miss school. That's what you think, isn't it?"

"Maybe."

"Well, you're wrong. I know what I want, and it can't be found in a Manhattan television studio, or any television studio."

"Where can it be found?"

"Maybe I'll tell you some time. Right now, if you'll excuse me, I think I'll go for a run so I can work off some excess steam before I call Jerry."

Paul stopped at his house after his run, to shower and shave before he came back to use Pam's phone. She, meantime, tugged on jeans and a sweater.

Jerry Bernstein wasn't in his office on Paul's first try. It was nearly ten by the time client and agent connected, and by then, whatever steam Paul had worked off while jogging was building to a full head again.

Pam was curled up on the couch working on the crossword puzzle from the Sunday *Boston Globe* when Paul finally got Jerry on the phone, so she couldn't help but hear Paul's side of the conversation.

"That's a damned lie," Paul snapped angrily. "I never told Sid Brown or anyone else that I'd sign the new contract if they agreed to write me out of the script for long enough to let Griffith go off on his mercy mission. If Sid's saying that, it's just so much—"

Obviously, Jerry cut in fast, but from the expression on Paul's face Pam couldn't tell whether he was being placated or chastised by his agent.

Then he snarled, "I'm not hearing you, Bernstein. No... you listen to me. I've had enough of the whole damned charade, understand? I appreciate everything you've done for me, but I think our relationship has been pretty fair. We've both come out on the plus side. Now I intend to cut out while I still have some of my sanity left. If everyone keeps on like this, all I can say is I'm going to be pushed into a premature case of memory loss."

Paul's smile was wicked. "If I can't remember my lines I can't say them, right?"

Pam could imagine Jerry Bernstein's frustration. She was actually feeling sorry for Paul's agent when Paul finally hung up.

He immediately turned to her. "Let's get out of here and see what's going on over the border, all right?" he suggested. Then he added quickly, "If you're up to a small safari, that is?"

"I'm up to it."

There was no problem crossing the border into Canada. Paul and Pam merely had to assert that they were American citizens and state their places of birth.

They spent the next few hours driving around back roads in the province of Quebec, mostly through rural areas. The quaint ambience—like the signs in French— lent interest to the trip. When they stopped at a bakery in a small village, the *boulanger* spoke no English, and Pam had fun using her high school French to purchase a loaf of freshly baked bread.

As they headed back to the States, they munched on the bread and drank apple cider that they'd bought at a farm.

It was nearly dark when they got back to Bryant Lake, and as he pulled up in front of her cottage, Paul said, "This time I'm not going to ask you to invite me in. You look tired. . . ."

"Are you going to tell me again that I need to get some sleep?"

"Yep."

He was right. But it was hard for Pam to slip out of the Trooper and watch him drive off. Since yesterday, she'd spent every minute with him, and it felt strange to be alone again.

Come on, she chided herself. Nothing like yesterday's apt to happen again, nor would you want it to.

Still, a bittersweet sadness settled over Pam as she went onto the porch, curled up in one of the blue chairs and rocked to and fro until a cool breeze sent her inside.

The moon was nearly full and there was a silvery cast to the woods as she got ready for bed.

Silver reminded her of Paul's eyes. Moonlight, in turn, symbolized romance. She wished she could share tonight's moonlight with Paul.

For that matter . . . she wished she could share everything with Paul. Forever and ever.

Chapter Seven

"Am I interrupting something?"

Paul stood on Pam's porch, looking terrific in a bright blue running suit.

For the past two hours, Pam had been trying to concentrate on working out a plan to deal with the many thick notebooks that comprised her father's journal. Thoughts of Paul had raised havoc with her discipline. And now that he was standing before her in person, he was raising added havoc.

"Pam?" he queried.

"Oh," Pam managed to say. "Yes. I mean, no. You're not interrupting anything. Come on in."

He followed her into the living room and saw the work area she'd set up for herself. "Looks like you're into something," he observed. "You should have told me to bug off."

"I wasn't getting anywhere," she confessed.

He eyed the journals curiously. "What are you up to? Or don't you want to say?"

She smiled. "What I'm doing—what I'm trying to do—isn't exactly top secret. My father started to keep a journal when he was twelve years old. His aunt gave him the first of the notebooks you see there as a birthday present. Once he started, he kept on going."

"How many are there?"

"Twenty-six. He kept making entries until shortly before he died, when he was almost fifty-four. He started writing at the end of World War II, and kept going through the Korean War, Vietnam and most of the eighties. He was an astute scene perceiver, even when he was very young. His observations make fascinating reading...."

"So that's what you're doing? Rereading your father's story of his life?"

"That's only part of it. A publisher in western Massachusetts who was a good friend of my father's has seen some of this material and he wants me to write a book based on the journals. Not a strict biography of my father, but more of a reminiscence of several vital decades of the country's history as seen through his eyes."

"Is that why you came to Bryant Lake, Pam? To work on the book?"

"That was a big part of my reason. I came up here to try to pull my thoughts together and decide on the right way to go with Dad's story," she said. "I wangled a three-month leave of absence from the paper—granted mainly because my present publisher is also interested in this project. He wants the first chance to publish excerpts from the book."

Pam sighed. "Right now—" she waved toward the journals "—the idea of putting all that together staggers me. I guess that's why I've been so slow about even taking the journals out of the three briefcases I lugged them up from Boston in."

"I guess I haven't helped," Paul said ruefully. "I've taken up your time."

"You also saved my life," Pam reminded him. "There'd be no book if you hadn't been around when I decided to take that icy swim in the lake. Anyway... I know this'll come on as an excuse but I just don't seem to be able to put myself in the right mood. Too many cobwebs cluttering up my brain, I guess."

"I can relate to that." Paul stood, stretched and said, "Regardless, I should leave you alone and give you a chance to try again."

"I don't know. I'm... restless," Pam admitted. "I've been wishing the journals were on tape so I could listen to them instead of reading them. I think maybe hearing the words would get me into the spirit faster."

"Want me to read to you?"

The offer was tempting, very tempting. Pam pictured Paul here with her, reading to her, and she knew she could listen to his voice forever.

But work was a way to separate herself from Paul. Every time they were together very long, her emotional risk increased. This time at Bryant Lake was transitory. When this interlude was over, she'd be going in one direction and he'd be going in another.

The thought of their turning their backs on each other once they returned to their own worlds was indescribably painful.

Pam said, "I couldn't possibly ask you to read to me, Paul. You're here on a vacation, after all, and..."

"This isn't exactly what I'd call a vacation," Paul said. "I'm here to come to grips with a lot of things. Though writing a book's your rationale, I think the same pretty much applies to you. Anyway—" he grinned "—one thing I *can* do is read lines. I've had a lot of experience. How about auditioning me?"

Pam laughed. "I don't need an audition. You're hired."

A little while later, Pam curled up in a corner of the couch and Paul started to read the first of the journals. She was astonished by the life he brought to her father's pages.

He'd insisted he wasn't really an actor. Regardless, he read beautifully, spacing the words, handling the phrases, interjecting just enough color and emotion, so that she had the uncanny feeling her father was speaking to her.

She lost track of time as she listened to Paul read about her father's life when he was growing up in a town in the Berkshires. Joshua Martin's introduction to the newspaper business had been via his job as a paper boy for the *Berkshire Eagle.* He also worked in a local grocery store on Saturdays, and for a time it looked as though he'd have to drop out of high school and get a full-time job to help contribute to his family's sagging finances.

But for all of the hard times, the scrounging to get by, there'd been a warm and loving spirit in the Martin family. It was that kind of spirit, Pam knew, that had stayed with her father all his life, and he'd passed along some of the good things he'd learned to her.

She was startled when Paul suddenly stopped reading and stuck an index card into the journal to mark his place before he closed the book.

"That's the end of a segment," he said, "and I don't think my strength will hold out unless I get something to eat. I'm starving."

Pam glanced at the clock and felt guilty. It was well past noontime; Paul had been reading for two hours.

"I'll fix sandwiches and soup," she offered.

Pam led the way into the kitchen, where she prepared and served the light meal.

As they ate, she said, "Thanks, Paul. I'm actually beginning to feel inspired."

"Great."

"I think I can take it from here."

He slanted a quizzical glance toward her. "Does that mean I'm fired?"

"It means I'm letting you off the hook."

He finished a second tuna fish-salad sandwich, then said, "Suppose I don't want to get off the hook?" She started to speak. "No, hear me out, Pam. I really enjoyed it. I wish I'd known your father."

Pam thought about that. Would her father and Paul have hit it off together? They were very different, yet...

"I wish you had," she said.

"He was just a kid when he wrote some of that stuff, but I'd say he was a very keen observer of the human scene even then," Paul reflected. "He conveys a real feeling of what was going on. I get a good idea of the sense of values he and his family had. Maybe his parents were broke, maybe he had to work harder than he should have—but they gave him love and understanding. They taught him how to care, wouldn't you say?"

Touched, Pam murmured, "Yes, I'd say so."

"I never had anything like that." There was a faraway look in Paul's eyes. "No firm foundation to build a life on. It's a lack I don't think anyone can entirely compensate for. At least . . . everything I learned I had to learn the hard way."

Pam asked gently, "Is your mother still living?"

He stared at his empty coffee cup. "I doubt it. She had me when she was pretty young—she wouldn't be more than early fifties even now. But the way she was going, she was burning out before I even ran away. Friday paychecks meant getting drunk and having a rip-roaring time raising hell . . . with me, and my stepbrothers and sisters, among other things. My stepfather, I have to say, never laid a hand on us. But she beat up on us, especially me . . . she resented the hell out of me."

"God," Pam breathed, imagining that she could feel his pain and wishing she could make up to him, somehow, for his terrible childhood.

"That was a long time ago, Pam," he said, as if reading her thoughts. "When I was still pretty young, I taught myself not to look back, and ordinarily I never do. When you start out life the way I did, there's no middle course. You go up, or you go down. I was determined to go up."

"And you did."

"I like to think so."

"I wonder about something," Pam mused after a moment. "Once you became so famous, don't you think your mother would have tried to contact you if she were still alive? Or your stepbrothers and sisters, for that matter?"

"I doubt very much if my mother would have recognized me by the time I got on TV," Paul said flatly. "I was a skinny kid when I left home, still at the acne stage. As for my stepbrothers and sisters . . . they were all a lot younger than I am. They certainly wouldn't have recognized me—especially as Jason St. Clair.

"That's one reason why I was so willing to go along with Jerry and his plans," he added. "I wanted a complete change of identity. The last thing I ever would have wanted was for my past to catch up with me. Now the danger's long over."

He was right. Some of his family members were probably still alive, but their world would be so far separated from his there could be no crossing at this late date. That seemed very sad to her.

"Don't," Paul said suddenly.

"Don't what?"

"Don't look like that, sweetheart. I grew up. I think I pretty well got rid of any emotional scars. I'm fine. True, nothing in the world could compel me to write down the story of *my* life. I view my life as a series of closed books, but I can say honestly that each book has turned out better than the last. Now, once I get rid of the latest book, the future..."

"Yes?" Pam prompted.

"I like to think that'll be a whole new story."

He pushed back from the table. "Speaking of books—how about getting back to work?"

"You've had enough for one day."

"I have? Or have you had enough?" he teased. "You don't have to answer that. I agree, let's call it quits for now. Why don't we go somewhere?"

The world outside the kitchen windows was gray. Pam said, "Looks like it's going to start to pour any minute."

"So? We can put on our foul-weather gear."

"Yes," she decided. "Yes. There's a special place I want to show you."

Paul drove the Trooper, but Pam did the navigating. They traveled along the lake, heading away from the town, until finally Pam said, "There it is. See that road on the left?"

Paul peered through the windshield. "You call that a road?"

"Yes. Go ahead and make the turn. I've done this in a regular car. It should be no problem with a four-wheel drive."

Paul turned, and almost immediately they came to a sharp jog to the right. The road began to climb, getting steeper and steeper.

Finally Paul ground the Trooper to a halt. "Looks like the end of the line," he said. "What's here?"

They were in the middle of a thickly wooded area. Bushes, vines and brambles surrounded them.

"Turning around's apt to be a problem," Paul warned.

"You don't turn around here," Pam informed him. "Keep going—see that jog to the left?"

"I'll take your word for it."

"I—er—I don't think anyone's been up here for a while," Pam admitted. "Things look a lot more overgrown than they were last time I was here."

"And when was that?"

"Oh, maybe six or seven years ago."

"You still think if I make a left turn through that gap we're going to wind up somewhere?"

"I know we are."

"This proves the kind of confidence I have in you, lady," Paul said. "I doubt my eyes, but not your wisdom. So, here goes."

The gap between the trees was so narrow that the Trooper could barely get through it. But, to Pam's relief, the road she remembered was still there. A little the worse for wear, but still navigable for a vehicle like this one.

"We may be on our way to heaven," Paul suggested, as he shifted gears and the car continued to ascend.

"We are," Pam said happily. "In fact, we're almost there."

They topped a rise as she spoke, and ahead and to their right was a clearing. "Pull in," she exclaimed. "Oh, this is just the way it was. I was so afraid this might have changed. Paul, this is the most beautiful spot in the world."

She met his eyes as she spoke, and discovered that he was staring at her so intently she couldn't possibly have said another word.

He said softly, "I've never known anyone like you. All right, Pam, show me the most beautiful place in the world."

Paul parked the vehicle and Pam led him across the clearing, then along a narrow trail through the woods that suddenly opened upon a mountain lake rimmed by dark green pines. On this sunless day, the water reflected the darkness of the pines and the pale gray of the sky. Near shore were several large gray boulders that looked as though they must have been dropped by a celestial giant who'd grown tired of playing with them. Still closer, a fallen tree arced into the water, its trunk silvered by time and the weather.

The air was still; there was not a sound until Pam murmured very softly, "It's just the two of us, at the very top of the world."

Paul was standing behind her, and Pam held her breath as his arms stole around her waist. "Does this place have a name?"

"Lost Lake," she said, keeping her voice very low as if it might be sacrilege to speak any louder. "I saw it first on a day like this. My father and I were exploring and we came upon it. Later, an old man my father knew told him the name. The road was better then than it is now. Even so...it was remote. I don't think many people have even known it's here.

"There's something eerie and wonderful about the grayness...."

"Yes, there is." Paul's voice was husky. "Thank you for sharing it with me."

Pam said slowly, "I never thought I'd share it with anyone. It's...very special and private to me."

"Then I thank you all the more. Especially because you're very special to me."

Pam held her breath as Paul turned her in his arms and brushed his lips across her forehead. She quivered as he nuzzled her cheekbone, then found the soft sweetness of the hollow behind her ear and explored it with his tongue. Delight spiraled; deep sensations surged. Dear God, she loved him so much.... And if this was insanity she'd as soon be crazy forever.

He held her, resting his chin against her curly blond hair, and she both heard and felt him draw in a very deep breath. The brakes again?

The rain had been holding off, but now the first drops began to fall. Pam felt the cool beads, heard Paul say, "I guess we're about to find out how waterproof we are."

There was no way anyone could have sprinted along the path back to the clearing. It was too rough and uneven. As it was, they grasped hands and stumbled along back to the Trooper, and the exertion helped slacken the sensual tension strung between them like a thin, tight wire.

Pam let Paul concentrate on driving as he wove down and around the steep and narrow curves that led back to the main road.

"I wouldn't be too crazy about doing that after another hour or so of rain," he admitted, once they were paralleling Bryant Lake again. "It would be a muddy, slippery mess. But I'm glad the way to Lost Lake is just as it is."

"You are?"

"Yes. I'm glad most people around here nowadays don't remember the lake, or how to get to it. It makes me feel like it's ours. Being there . . . It's a hard experience to describe."

Pam nodded. She knew exactly what he meant.

"Pam?"

"What?"

"Last time you were there," Paul asked, "were you with your father?"

"No, matter of fact I wasn't," she recalled. "My father was busy with an editorial he was writing. That was not long before he had to bow out of the newspaper business. It was a day like today, and I drove up to the lake alone."

"You shared a lot around here with your father, though, didn't you?"

"Yes. Bryant Lake was our special place."

"Weren't there other people, too?"

"What do you mean?"

"You only talk about your father."

"I suppose that's because this *was* our special place, and it's the first time I've been back since . . . he's been gone," she said. "But, I was never just a daddy's girl.

The mere thought of that would have horrified my father. If anything, he was always urging me to expand my horizons.''

"Did you follow his advice?''

"To a point, though maybe not as much as he wanted me to. I think he would have had me traveling to all corners of the globe. He would have missed me a lot, I know that. But that's the way he was. He never put himself first.''

"Did he like the men in your life?''

She shrugged. "Some yes, some no. I don't think he was all that crazy about any of them, but I was never very serious about anyone, either.''

"Until Alfred?''

She frowned. Hearing Alfred's name reminded her that she hadn't gotten back to Linda yet. The past two nights, she'd needed all the rest she could get. Paul had been right. Sleep was nature's way of healing.

But she couldn't avoid calling Linda much longer. She'd have to phone her tonight, though she didn't want to. Linda would only stir up a lot of things she didn't want to think about just now.

She said, "My father never knew Alfred.''

"That's not exactly what I asked,'' Paul pointed out, and then let it go. "Wasn't your father even interested in remarrying?''

"No,'' Pam said softly. "I often wished someone else would come into his life, but it was pretty clear he never wanted to take anyone into it. He loved my mother so much there could never be anyone else for him.''

"That's the way I'd be if . . .'' Paul began. Then, after a pause, he finished, "If I ever really fell in love.''

"Linda?''

"Don't tell me!'' Linda Bailey retorted coldly.

Pam was afraid her friend was about to hang up on her. She said hastily, "Look, I had every intention of getting back to you sooner, but something happened."

"Like what?" Linda asked skeptically.

"I nearly drowned in the middle of the lake."

Shock rendered Linda speechless. Pam took the opportunity to fill her in with details of the episode.

"Who was this man who saved you?" Linda immediately demanded.

"He has a cottage down the lake from me. He just happened to be out jogging—which was very lucky for me. Linda, whatever you do, don't mention anything about this to Alfred." She was thinking about Angela Santoro hiring a team of private detectives. If Alfred became sufficiently aroused he could resort to the same ploy, undoubtedly with considerably more success. She'd made no overwhelming effort to cover her trail after leaving Boston.

"Believe me, I don't even speak to Alfred Beverly unless I'm forced to," Linda said. "As a matter of fact, I've been thinking about turning in my letter of resignation tomorrow."

"You can't be serious."

"Oh, yes, I'm serious. Alfred knows damned well I know where you are, and he's been making my life so miserable I have an anxiety attack each morning when I wake up and think about going to work."

"Linda, I'm sorry. I'm honestly sorry."

"What I don't understand," Linda said fretfully, "is why Alfred hasn't figured out for himself where you are."

"He doesn't know about my cottage," Pam confessed.

"That seems strange."

"Not really. Alfred actually doesn't know most of my friends—people I've let use the cottage since Dad died, and I haven't been coming up here myself. We've never really traveled in the same circles."

"And this is the man you're going to marry?" Linda moaned. "To think I'm responsible. I wish I'd never introduced the two of you."

Pam said gently, "Alfred is not the man I'm going to marry."

"Whew! Does Alfred know that?"

"No."

"When are you going to tell him? It may make a lot of difference to my professional future. If he succumbs to sorrow for a while, maybe he'll mellow out."

Pam made a decision. "I'll call him and tell him now."

"Over the phone?" Linda was horrified.

"No. I couldn't do that, could I?" Pam sighed. "I'll talk to Alfred and set up a meeting in Boston."

"Just let me know when you're coming, will you?" Linda urged. "I want to be sure I'm not around."

Pam paced the floor restlessly after she'd finished her conversation with Linda, dreading having to dial Alfred's number. But finally she convinced herself that putting off the call wasn't going to make it any easier.

Alfred answered on the second ring, and when he heard her voice there was stark silence at his end of the line.

"Alfred?" Pam asked when the silence persisted.

"Where are you?" Alfred demanded.

"Where I've been all along," she answered evasively. "And, before you ask, I'm fine."

"That's more than I can say for myself."

"Alfred...I'm sorry. I can appreciate how you must feel."

"Can you?"

"I needed to put some distance between us, for both our sakes," Pam tried to explain.

"Well, has this interlude brought you to your senses?"

"I think so, yes."

"In that event—"

"I'd like to have lunch with you Friday," Pam cut in. "How about Jacob Wirth's at one o'clock?"

"What?"

"I asked you if—"

"I know what you asked me. But I don't think our minds are meeting, Pam. I was about to discuss our setting a date for the wedding and you're suggesting..."

"We need to talk, Alfred."

"I'm not sure I like the sound of that."

"Jacob Wirth's. One o'clock. Friday," Pam said.

She hung up before Alfred could answer her.

Chapter Eight

Pam woke up Thursday morning wishing it were Saturday. Then her rendezvous with Alfred would be over and she could go on with the rest of her life.

A steady rain was speckling the lake. The air was damp and chilly. Pam shivered as she stood on the back porch, staring at nothing in particular. Today's gray world was not at all like the wonderful, eerie atmosphere she'd shared yesterday with Paul at Lost Lake. Because she was facing it alone? It daunted her to think how much being with Paul had come to mean to her.

She felt moody and depressed as she went back inside, picked up her father's first notebook and tried to resume reading the story where Paul had left off. Soon she set the notebook aside. Her problem was not only that she wished Paul were here reading to her, but she missed his interpretation as well. He made her father's words come alive.

As the morning passed, Pam hoped Paul would come over. He'd seemed interested in the reading project he'd volunteered for. She guessed she'd more or less taken it for granted that he'd want to continue. But the hours went by, and he didn't appear.

Meantime, Pam bagged the idea of doing any more reading herself and, instead, huddled with her portable electronic typewriter and tried to concentrate on blocking out a working outline.

There were numerous options, but she couldn't decide on any one of them.

By early afternoon, Pam was suffering from acute cabin fever and she knew she had to get out. Her eyes fell on a collection of games on the bottom bookcase shelf. Scrabble, cribbage, backgammon...maybe Paul would enjoy playing one of them? She doubted if he'd be out on a day like this. Would he welcome some company?

He'd been somewhat remote when they'd parted. But this was a new day, and an especially dreary one. Pam watched the rain spatter against her windowpanes and decided she *was* Paul's neighbor, after all. She liked to think she also was his friend. There was no logical reason why she shouldn't pay him a visit.

She put on her rain gear, tucked the Scrabble game into a plastic bag and started out.

The rain was coming down harder than ever as she neared Paul's house. She tugged her slicker hood down, made a run for it and dashed up to his front door. Had her vision not been partly obscured by the hood, she realized later, she would have seen the dark sedan parked farther along the road.

"Hi," she began when Paul opened the door. Pam was so happy to see him that she gave him her widest smile. But then the smile froze in place as she saw the expression on his face.

He was looking at her as if she might as well be from another planet.

Pam took an involuntary step backward and nearly fell off the stoop. Paul grabbed her arm.

"Pam," he said. "Come on in."

Paul tugged Pam inside his living room, and she stood on the edge of the rug, her raincoat dripping.

Then she became aware that they were not alone.

A short, plump man who looked like a middle-aged cherub pushed himself up from one of the chintz-covered armchairs.

Paul, still seeming somewhat distracted, made introductions. "Pam," he said, "this is Jerry Bernstein. Jerry, this is Pamela Martin."

Paul's agent blinked when he heard her name. "Martin?" he queried. "Are you two related?"

Paul considered that for a moment, then he slanted a rather odd smile in Pam's direction. "Related?" he echoed. "Maybe we are . . . in a way."

Before Pam could respond to that, he added, "Let me take your raincoat."

"No," Pam said hastily. "I . . . I have to get back."

Paul's smile assumed that teasing quality she knew so well. "You just got here, Pam," he reminded her.

"I know. But I'm only allowing myself a short break. I needed a little fresh air and exercise. I just stopped by to see how you were doing."

"What's in the bag?"

Pam stared down at the plastic bag she was still holding. "A Scrabble game."

Paul took it from her hand, which suddenly seemed to have gone limp. Then he slid her raincoat off her shoulders and said, "I'll hang this out back."

Pam made a last effort. "Really," she said, "I should go. Anyway, I'm sure you and Mr. Bernstein have a lot to say to each other."

"We've already said most of it," Paul commented, as he exited toward the kitchen. "Right, Jerry?"

Jerry Bernstein shrugged. "Why ask me?"

He looked moody as he watched Paul leave the room. Then he turned to Pam. "You live around here?"

"Just down the road."

"You stay here year-round?"

"No. I live in Boston most of the time."

"Boston, eh?" Jerry Bernstein seemed to be trying to make some connection between his client and a woman who lived in Boston.

Paul came back, and reported almost casually, "Jerry's been trying to convince me to go back to New York with him." He added, "Don't look so startled, Jerry. Pam knows all about me, but my secret's safe with her."

As she heard Paul say that, Pam's heart began to sing.

"After he finished talking to me yesterday, Jerry decided we weren't going to get anywhere over the phone so he drove up here," Paul went on. "For Jerry, making a pilgrimage this far from Manhattan is like taking off for the moon. He pulled in at three o'clock this morning, we talked till seven, snatched some sleep . . . and here we are."

"Nowhere," Jerry Bernstein asserted gloomily.

"I don't know about that," Paul said cheerfully. "If you've been listening to what I've been saying, you should pretty much know where I stand, Jerry."

"I haven't heard anything I hadn't already heard before. I still can't buy it."

Paul considered that, then said, "There's another factor, Pam. Jerry found me without any trouble. Now he thinks the investigators Angela's hired will be able to do the same thing. I'm trying to convince him it was easy for him because he—basically—knew where I was. He knew I had a cottage on Bryant Lake." Paul grinned. "Lucky he hit my mailbox first with the name Martin on it, or you'd have had a rude awakening."

Was it her imagination, or did Paul seem more relaxed than he had a few minutes ago? Did he actually like having her here? Was she good for him?

Paul said, "I fired up the wood stove because Jerry was freezing to death."

She nodded. "It's nice and warm in here."

He settled down in one of the armchairs. "Jerry," he urged, "stop looking like we're about to be invaded by aliens from some forbidden planet. Believe me, there's no way Angela's men are going to be able to pick up my trail."

"I don't know why you're so damned sure about that," Jerry Bernstein muttered.

"Because I covered my tracks very carefully."

"So you covered your tracks. Maybe a couple of good private eyes could uncover them. What I'm trying to make you see is that I don't want Angela to get the jump on this. If she finds you, she'll build the whole thing into her own publicity stunt. And if there's going to be publicity, I'd like it to come from us."

"There's not going to be any publicity. Not, that's to say, until you make up your mind to tell the producers either Griffith McQueen has to die or they're going to need to find another guy who looks just like me."

"Come off it, Jace."

Jace? Yes, Pam remembered, Jerry Bernstein was the one who'd given Paul the name Jason St. Clair.

Paul said, "Just to convince you that no one's going to find me until I want to be found, suppose I fill you in on the story of my daring escape."

Jerry groaned, but Pam leaned forward, interested.

"I left my condo in Manhattan and drove up to Angela's place in Connecticut," Paul began.

Jerry's head shot up. *"What?"*

Paul turned to Pam. "Angela has a summer place on the shore in Connecticut. Usually she throws a big party there just before the start of each new season for everyone connected with the show. She seldom goes up after that. But, frankly, I'm not as adverse to her capitalizing on any publicity she can milk from my walking out as Jerry is. I figure sooner or later she'll discover the car, sound the alarm, and that will be okay with me."

Jerry groaned again. "She finds your car, she calls the cops, they're going to think you went for a long swim in the Sound."

Paul shrugged. "Let them. Eventually, I'll emerge. Anyway—just for the record, Jerry, Angela's garage was locked. I broke the lock. No big deal. Tell Angela sometime that she should install a decent security system."

"I can see the headlines." Jerry looked miserable. "Angela Santoro's Rejection Pushes Jason St. Clair To Suicide." Jerry traced imaginary words in the air with his index finger. "TV Star's Car Found In Leading Lady's Connecticut Garage," he continued. "That kind of juicy publicity should be enough to get Angela a raise. I should be *her* agent!"

Jerry sighed. "Pamela. You don't mind if I call you Pamela?"

"No."

"You have some influence on this guy. Use it," Jerry Bernstein pleaded. "Convince him he can't hide for the rest of his life."

Pam avoided Paul's silvery eyes as she said, "I don't have any influence with Paul. There's no reason why I should. But you're right, Jerry. No one can hide for-ever—not without giving up a great deal."

"Listen to her," Jerry urged his client.

"I'll listen later," Paul said, with a gleam in his eye that wasn't lost on Pam. "Meantime—aren't the two of you eager to hear the rest of my escape story?"

"Tremendously eager," Jerry said wearily.

Paul settled back. "Over a period of time," he said, "I snitched some stuff from the costume department at the studio. A couple of wigs. Some clothes I wouldn't ordinarily wear. I changed in Angela's garage into some ratty jeans and an old sweater. They'd been worn in one of the episodes by a guy who played the part of a drifter. I put on a dark red wig, took out the contacts, put my glasses on. Hell . . . I even felt like a different person.

"I hiked cross-country from Angela's place to a state road, then I hitched to Hartford. I changed into an-other outfit and put on another wig in the men's room at the Hartford bus station, and dumped the stuff I'd been wearing in a trash can. Then I took a bus to Bur-lington.

"I stayed in Burlington for a couple of days. By then, I knew the trail was really cold. So I rented a car and drove across the state to Bryant Lake. I wasn't too fussy about shaving or getting a haircut. For that matter, no one's ever recognized me in Bryant Lake, anyhow. Until..."

Paul stopped, and Pam was sure he'd been about to say, "Until you did, Pam."

Why had he cut himself short?

She suddenly remembered how grubby Paul had looked that first time she'd seen him in Cullum's store. Since then, he'd been shaving regularly and combing his hair. Because of her?

It was a heady thought.

Jerry said, "You may be right. Maybe Angela's private eyes won't be able to find you. That still doesn't change what I said. You can't go on hiding forever."

"I have no intention of hiding forever, Jerry. You know my conditions. Once you finalize my severance from *When Tomorrow Comes* I'll join the world again. I even promise to go along with whatever story you invent to explain my disappearance. Hell—I'll even bluff my way through amnesia, if you want me to."

Jerry scowled. "I don't want to make up stories—no one would believe them, anyway. The problem is, you're cutting your own nose off. That's what worries me. Sid Brown says you made a verbal agreement with him that you'd come back on the show if he'd get the scriptwriters to keep Griffith offstage for the first few segments in the new season. They've done that. Now time is running out. The ratings are already going down without Griffith on the show. The sponsors are raising hell—"

"Not my problem."

"Pamela," Jerry pleaded, "say something to him, will you?"

"You're overestimating my influence," Pam objected, "but I will say one thing. He's right, Paul."

Paul glowered. "Traitor!"

"You need to go back. Face reality, one way or another."

"You don't know what you're saying. Those people are vultures."

"I imagine you could deal with vultures on your own terms if you wanted to," Pam said evenly. "You certainly have the upper hand. They'll make any kind of concessions in order to get you back."

Paul's eyes locked with hers. "Are you saying you'd like me to reincarnate Griffith McQueen, M.D.?"

"He isn't dead, Paul."

"The hell he isn't. Jason St. Clair killed him when he left his car in Angela Santoro's garage."

Pam frowned. "You're talking in riddles."

"No, I'm not. That was the last act Jason St. Clair will ever perform because he's dead, too. Witness Paul Martin, who has risen from the ashes."

"The guy's crazy, Pamela," Jerry muttered.

Paul ignored that. He said to Pam, "Anyway, who are you to talk? Have you forgotten that you also dropped out? I don't see you about to go back and give yourself up."

Jerry looked intrigued.

This was not the moment, Pam decided, to tell Paul she was going to Boston tomorrow to meet Alfred and inform him she couldn't marry him. She said stiffly, "My situation's entirely different from yours."

"Is it?" Paul drawled. "Seems to me in each case we're facing up to decisions that will profoundly affect the rest of our lives."

Pam just looked at him, and after a minute Jerry said, "I don't think the lady wants to get into that, Jace."

She was grateful to Paul's agent, who right now seemed to have more perception than Paul did.

The small lull that followed gave her needed time. She managed, without stumbling over the words, to say, "I have to get back to work—we'll leave Scrabble for another day."

Paul followed her to the door after she'd bid Jerry goodbye. "Did you go on with the notebook we were reading yesterday?" he asked her, his voice low, intended for her ears only.

"Not very far," she admitted.

"Good. Jerry's going to stick around through tonight, but he'll be taking off for the city first thing tomorrow morning. Why don't you bring a couple of the notebooks over and we can spend the day reading? I'll make that moussaka I promised you."

"I have to go to Boston tomorrow, and it'll be late when I get back. Maybe Saturday?"

Paul only nodded, but Pam caught the expression in his eyes. He'd told his agent just a short while ago that his secret was safe with her. But now, Pam suspected he was beginning to doubt his own word. She'd never seen anyone look more skeptical.

Maybe if he had come out and asked her why she was going to Boston she would have told him, she thought, as she dodged raindrops on the way home.

But he hadn't asked.

Alfred was waiting at Jacob Wirth's when Pam got there. He was at a table along the wall, nursing a glass of imported German beer.

He stood as she approached, and Pam felt as though she were seeing him for the first time. Alfred made a fantastic initial impression. He wasn't handsome in the way Paul was, but he both looked and acted like the successful executive he was.

He was wearing a dark gray suit, a pale gray shirt and a tie striped in crimson, black and oyster white. Even the touches of gray at his temples were exactly right.

Alfred would age gracefully. Pam couldn't imagine seeing him rumpled and unshaven. On the other hand, she'd seen Paul with old clothes on, stubble on his face, his rumpled hair in need of a cut, and he'd still been so devastatingly sexy that...

She shut off a very disturbing image of Paul and ordered a glass of wine, aware that Alfred's keen dark eyes were analyzing her. She knew how sharp he was. He was taking in every aspect of her, and she wondered how she was measuring up.

"You don't look as if you've had much rest lately," he finally diagnosed.

She'd had bad dreams since nearly drowning the other day. In the middle of the night, she would wake up feeling as if she were going under again, as if she were being pulled beneath the surface of the lake by strong, icy fingers. But then she'd come back up and Paul would be holding her in a warm embrace. . . .

"I'm fine," she said shortly.

"Pamela—I can't help but wonder why you chose this particular place for us to meet."

Pam looked around the old German restaurant that was a Boston institution. The ceiling was very high, the walls cream colored above dark wood paneling. There was a sprinkling of sawdust on the floor. No soft lights and hidden corners here, but an open atmosphere which offered little chance for real privacy.

She'd selected the less-than-intimate ambience deliberately.

"I thought it would be convenient for both of us," she hedged.

Alfred leaned back, and weariness and exasperation mixed in his voice as he asked, "Just what is this all about? I think I have a right to know why you decided you needed to run away from me. Here we are, engaged..."

"We are not engaged, Alfred," Pam reminded him.

"We might as well be."

"No, that's not so. Oh, God." She looked at Alfred helplessly. "There's no easy way to say this," she confessed. "Believe me, I don't want to hurt you. But I can't marry you. That's the reason I went away. So I could make an objective decision. Well...I've made it."

She waited for a reaction. Nothing happened. She'd been studying the sawdust on the floor. Now she glanced quickly at Alfred and saw that his face was perfectly blank.

"I wasn't aware that you've been under such a strain," he said. "You're exhausted. Anyone can see that." He looked at his watch. "Jud Haverson should be in his office in half an hour or so. I'll call him. I'm sure he'll fit you into his schedule. I'll go over with you."

"Who is Jud Haverson?"

"My doctor."

"A shrink?"

"No. Jud is an internist."

"Why do you think I need to see a doctor?"

"I believe I just explained that," Alfred stated patiently. "Your nerves are on edge, you need rest and probably a tranquilizer to settle you down...."

"I don't need rest and I don't need a tranquilizer." Why hadn't she ever seen how self-righteous Alfred was? "What I need," Pam said, "is for you to hear what I just said."

"I don't want to hear it, Pamela. You're not making sense. As a matter of fact, I thought when we left here we might go up to Shreve's and choose your ring. But that can wait until you've seen Jud."

The woman who married Alfred, Pam thought, would have her life beautifully arranged for her. She wouldn't even have to think if she didn't want to.

Acknowledging that calmed her down. She said quietly, "I've taken a three-month leave of absence from my job at the paper to write a book, Alfred. That's why I went away—part of the reason, anyhow. I wanted to work on the book, and to work out my feelings about you."

She went on, "I think I've accomplished both objectives. I've started on the book—at least I'm getting into it—and I know without a doubt that you and I were never meant for each other. Now...I'm sorry...but forgive me if I don't stay for lunch." She shook her head slightly, her blue eyes genuinely sorrowful as she looked at him. "I'm really sorry."

Pam was standing by the time she finished her speech. She wanted nothing so much as to get out, to get away, but there was one more' thing she had to say.'

"Let up on Linda," she advised, "or you'll lose one of the best account executives you've ever had. Neither she nor anyone else could influence my decision. I had to make it myself."

Pam turned on her heel and walked out.

She didn't have to look back to see whether or not Alfred had followed her. She knew he wouldn't follow her. He might be persistent and unyielding, but he was not a man who would humble himself.

Not much time would have to pass before Alfred began to rationalize their situation, Pam thought, as she headed toward the nearby parking garage where she'd left her car. He'd quickly convince himself that she was probably the most foolish woman he'd ever met, who had passed up her golden opportunity when she'd turned him down.

In fact, she suspected, before long Alfred probably would begin to feel that he'd had a narrow escape. And then it would be a simple matter to seek solace from someone else.

She switched on the car radio as she drove out of Boston, aiming for the network of highways that would take her back to Vermont.

The music program she turned to was interrupted for a station break, and then a news update.

Pam heard an announcer say, "Jason St. Clair, the television star reported missing earlier this month, has been discovered, unharmed, at a getaway cabin on a lake in northern Vermont. St. Clair, who has been living in remote Bryant Lake, a small community not far from the Canadian border, walked out on the production of the top-rated daytime drama, *When Tomorrow Comes,* at the start of the new television season.

"St. Clair's agent, Jerry Bernstein, was unavailable for comment."

Chapter Nine

Paul is going to blame me for this.

The words became a litany, a chant that silently repeated itself over and over again as the miles rolled under Pam's tires.

Paul, she remembered, had assured Jerry Bernstein yesterday that she'd keep his secret. But a little while later suspicion had flashed in his eyes when she'd said she was going to Boston.

The timing couldn't have been worse.

He'll think either I phoned my editor with the story and then made sure to get away while it broke, or that I took my story about him to Boston and the wire services did the rest.

By the time Pam reached the Vermont border, her nerves felt shredded.

Then, just south of Bradford, there was a tie-up on the interstate because of a major accident. When state police troopers finally waved her past the flashing lights and she saw the crumpled cars and the ambulance, she was thoroughly frazzled.

All the while, she'd kept the radio on, hoping for more details about Paul. But the announcer kept repeating a variation of the original bulletin each time the news was broadcast.

To make matters worse, it started to rain—this had to be the rainiest fall in Vermont history!—and Pam soon discovered her convertible's canvas top leaked. The windshield wiper didn't work too well, either.

Damned clunker of a car, she muttered.

The visibility was so poor that Pam had to keep her speed to a crawl for the last few miles, and once she'd pulled into her driveway she slumped over the wheel, exhausted.

She'd forgotten to bring a flashlight with her, and though the path to her door was familiar territory, she nevertheless stumbled and turned her ankle. As a final twist of fate, the key stuck in the lock, and by the time she got the door open, her hair was damp, her jacket was rain-spattered and her ankle hurt. She was close to tears, ready to let misery and frustration swamp her.

From somewhere in the darkness, a voice spoke.

"About time," Paul said.

He switched on a light and started toward her. Pam instinctively backed away, anything but ready for this confrontation.

Paul faced her, and she saw the anger stamped on his features.

"I wondered if you'd come back." He spoke casually, but there was nothing casual about the way he was looking at her. His gray eyes blazed with suppressed fury.

Pam gritted her teeth. Though she'd expected this kind of reaction from him, she'd done nothing to deserve it. She was innocent, dammit. She had the right to be heard before he condemned her.

She confronted the issue. "I heard the bulletin on the car radio."

"Fast work, wasn't it?" He was still using that casual, conversational tone. "I don't know if I'd rate page one in your paper, but I imagine your story will get a pretty good play in the morning edition. Too bad the radio beat you out. I talked to Jerry, and he tells me I made the national TV news. They dug out some studio stock shots of me and interviewed Angela.

"Also, thanks to state-of-the-art communication, a reporter from the *Vermont Mountaineer* got himself the print-media scoop. He turned up on my doorstep. But, of course, your version will be ever so much juicier. He didn't have that much to go on, nor did I help him out."

Pam tried to fight the ire and resentment. She needed to keep a cool head if she was going to convince him she'd had nothing to do with any of this. And unless she could make him believe her, believe *in* her . . .

She said tightly, "Before you leap to conclusions, you might consider some of the facts."

"Facts?" The question dripped scorn. "Come on, Pam, give me a break. The facts hit me right in the face a few hours ago. You ratted."

"You're sure of that, are you?" Pam clenched her fists so tightly that her fingernails dug into her palms. She was discovering that hate and love could actually collide.

Paul shrugged. "Why wouldn't I be?"

"Did it occur to you that maybe Jerry Bernstein was so fed up with your attitude he called a contact in New York when he got back?"

"I thought about that," Paul allowed. "But I don't think that's what happened."

"Why not?"

"Because it's to Jerry's disadvantage to have this come out right now. You must have gotten that message from him yesterday. As long as no one knew where I was, Jerry had some negotiating power. Jerry's the eternal optimist. Even after everything I'd said to him, he still hoped when he left here that he could switch my thinking so I'd consider going back on *When Tomorrow Comes* for one more season. All he was asking by then was that instead of signing a long-term contract, which is what the producers want, I compromise and agree to stay with the show until next summer's break. Jerry said he'd insist on a guarantee that they'd write Griffith out of the script in the last episode."

"But you didn't go along with that?"

"No. Granted, it would be a better deal than committing myself to another big chunk of time. But I don't want to commit myself to anything."

"So if it wasn't Jerry who turned you in it had to be me, is that it?"

"Who else?"

"How do I know? I'd think there are other people who could have done it. You've been shaving lately. What I'm saying is, anyone who ever watched you on TV very much could easily recognize you."

"You can't even get the show around here, so who could have seen me?"

"I don't know. You and I have eaten at a few places...."

"Out-of-the-way places. And I haven't exactly noticed us being followed, have you? Someone would have had to track me back here."

"All right. People see you at Cullum's store."

"I've been going up to Bert's first thing in the morning, right after he opens up. The only people around are a few old codgers who congregate to drink coffee and swap whoppers. I guarantee you not one of them has ever watched a soap opera in his entire life."

The high-heeled "city shoes" Pam had put on today were killing her feet. She kicked them off, then curled up in a corner of the couch. It was cold in the room. She shivered, then got up again and pattered toward the stone fireplace that had been her father's pride and joy. He had designed it himself.

She was so conscious of Paul's scrutiny that she nearly burned her fingers as she touched a match to kindling and crumpled newspapers, then fanned the blaze until the logs began to catch.

The fire of her anger began to die, leaving in its place a dull, hopeless ache, which was even worse. She tried to put herself in Paul's position, and wondered if she'd feel about him as he was feeling about her.

She doubted it. She was sure she'd have more faith in him.

She suspected that Paul's disillusionment went back to his early childhood. Fame probably hadn't helped, either. There was so much phoniness connected with being a celebrity. So many of the people who flocked around the famous were hangers-on.

Paul, she was beginning to conclude, didn't know much about real love or real friendship. Certainly he knew nothing at all about trust.

Pam went back to the couch and sat down. Then she said slowly, "I'm going to make one statement. If you can't accept what I say I'd like you to leave . . . because we'll have nothing further to talk about."

He waited.

"I did not give your story to anyone, I did not mention you or your whereabouts to anyone. Period."

The crackle of the fire on the hearth sounded very loud in the silence that followed.

Pam stared at the flames. She couldn't look at Paul. She felt too destroyed to face him. No one had ever hurt her like this before. His doubt, his total lack of faith in her, stabbed. The pain was real. She wanted to clutch her chest and rock back and forth and moan.

She said, "Leave, will you please?"

"No."

"Don't make me keep asking you, Paul. Just go."

"I'm not going to walk out now, Pam."

His voice was hoarse. The words seemed ripped from his throat.

She closed her eyes. "You've made yourself very clear," she said. "Now I want you out of here. This *is* my house. . . ."

That struck her. "How did you get in here in the first place?"

"You have a habit of locking your front door and leaving the kitchen door open. I came over by the path along the lake once the first reporter had left. I was pretty sure there'd be more, and I was right. I've been sitting by the window, watching—waiting for you, primarily. A TV mobile unit went by awhile ago. Big white truck. You couldn't miss it, even in the dark."

To her consternation, Paul crossed the stretch of floor that separated them and sat down much too close to her.

He reached for her hand. She pulled away from him.

"Don't," he said huskily. "Please don't. Instead of writing me off, try to understand, will you?"

Pam's laugh was short and bitter. "Aren't you mixing things up?"

He reached for her hand again; this time he took firm possession and wouldn't let go.

"Try to hear what I'm saying," he urged. "I want to believe you, Pam. But I can't."

The negation was all she needed to hear. "Great," she muttered, and tried to tug her hand away again. But Paul's grip tightened.

"Don't sound like that," he urged. "Oh, hell, how can I expect you to sound? I know how you must feel. All I can ask of you is to give me a little time."

"For what? So you work up a better case against me?"

"Why did you go to Boston?"

"Would you believe me if I told you?"

"You could try me, Pam."

"I'm not about to." Stung, the anger she'd felt earlier rekindled.

"Why should I let you do this to me?" she demanded. "You think I'm a liar and a cheat. Why should I try to convince you otherwise?"

"Please..."

"You *expect* people to let you down, don't you, Paul?"

His jaw muscle twitched. "Maybe I do."

"I get the idea every relationship you've ever had has been built on shifting sand."

"Maybe it has been. I've never let that get to me too much. A long time ago I learned to go it alone."

"Without caring for anyone?"

"I wouldn't say that."

"I would. I thought at least we were ... friends. But if you felt we had a valid friendship you'd know I'd never write a story about you that you didn't want written, and certainly I'd never tip anyone off about your being here in Bryant Lake."

"That's what Jerry said."

She slanted a quick glance at him. "Jerry said that?"

Paul nodded. "I called him shortly after I came over here. He'd just seen the news bulletin on TV. He was trying to figure out what to do."

"What did you suggest to him?"

"I told him to release a statement to the press and tell them the truth. I'm not going back to the show, and if the producers want to sue me because of a verbal agreement they allege I made they can go ahead."

"Did you make a verbal agreement with anyone?"

"No. You've heard both Jerry and me mention Sid Brown. Well, I talked to Sid when the contract negotiations started—quite awhile back now. If he thinks I made any verbal agreements, he's mistaken. He misunderstood me."

Paul finally released Pam's hand, and edged away from her. "Jerry's coming back up tomorrow," he said. "He's going to fly to St. Johnsbury and rent a car. After we've hashed over a few things, I'll go back to New York with him."

"You're going back?"

"Just long enough to make sure there won't be any legal hassles."

"What then?"

"I don't know what then," Paul said moodily. "The plans I've been trying to make are pretty much shot to hell right now. I'll have to let a little time pass and see what happens."

What plans had he been making? Pam was burning to ask him, but she wasn't about to. She wasn't going to chance his rebuff.

He said suddenly, "It's late. You must be tired. Why don't you go along to bed?"

"I intend to as soon as you leave," she informed him.

"I'm not leaving, Pam."

She stared at him. "You can't stay here, Paul."

"I have to," he said simply.

"You can't."

"I have to," he repeated. "There's no way I can go back to my place tonight. I'm not going anywhere, for that matter, till Jerry gets here."

"Paul, I can't let you stay here."

"There's no choice." His eyes and his tone were cool. "Believe me, Pam, you have nothing to worry about. Go to bed. I won't come within fifty feet of you."

"That's not the point. I don't want you here," Pam said, and for a moment almost believed herself. "I won't have you here. I know I can't evict you physically—"

He smiled a slow, lazy smile. "I'm glad you realize that."

"But I can call the police," Pam finished.

"The police hate to be called in on domestic squabbles, Pam. Usually they forego action and try to get away as fast as they can."

"This isn't a domestic squabble, dammit!"

"It would come across like one by the time I got through," he promised her.

She glared at him. "What an unpleasant person you can be!"

"What a stiff-necked little pain you can be!" Paul glanced at his watch. "It's almost midnight. Jerry should be calling any minute to firm up the plans for tomorrow. I think you'd better answer the phone in case some media genius has discovered another Martin living along the lake and starts trying to piece something together."

"Kindly stop trying to tell me what to do," Pam said, her eyes sparking. "If the phone rings you can damned well answer it."

The phone rang.

On the fifth ring, Pam said, "Will you kindly go pick up the receiver?"

"No. And I warn you Jerry will keep trying till he connects. The man doesn't know the meaning of giving up."

The third time the phone rang, Pam couldn't stand it any longer.

She barked her hello into the receiver and heard Jerry Bernstein ask, "Pamela?"

"Yes."

"Where's Jace?"

"Right here."

Pam went out to the kitchen after Paul took the phone from her. The rain was streaming down like water pouring out of an upturned celestial bucket. The whole damned place was going to be flooded, she thought gloomily. Maybe the lake would even rise enough to sweep all the cottages away, which might solve a lot of problems.

She sighed, got out a bottle of sherry and took it back into the living room, picking up a couple of glasses along the way.

Paul had concluded his conversation and was standing in front of the fire, having added another log. She handed him a glass of sherry and said, "I don't have anything stronger."

"Thanks," he murmured absently.

"Please drink it and then go home, all right?"

Paul's tone was patient. "Don't be childish."

"You really think that mobile TV truck's going to sit there all night waiting for you?"

He hunched his shoulders. "Who knows? News may be scarce."

He added, "Jerry should be here by late morning. He wants you to be here, too. He said he needs to talk to both of us."

"Oh, no," Pam retorted quickly. "I don't need to talk to Jerry, and I can't think of a reason in the world why I should do what he wants."

"Maybe because you owe me one," Paul suggested.

She frowned. "What are you talking about?"

"Earlier this week, lady, I saved your life, remember?"

"Of course I remember."

"Do you remember telling me you owed me one?"

"Yes," she admitted uncomfortably.

"Well, consider being here tomorrow when Jerry gets here part payment."

"*Part* payment?"

"Your life's worth more than a single meeting with me and my agent, isn't it?"

"Am I honestly supposed to answer that?" Pam protested. "Paul, this really *is* childish."

"On the contrary, you're the one who felt there was a debt involved. Now I'm going to ask you to pay up."

"What do you want me to do?"

"We can get into that tomorrow. For tonight...go to bed, will you, Pam?"

Paul looked tired, harassed, and unhappy. But Pam discovered that even under these less-than-favorable conditions his sexy charisma still packed a wallop that went right through her. Worse, she wanted to comfort him. She wanted to massage the worry lines from his forehead, ease the tension that tightened his lips...

Damn...the effect he had on her was insidious. If she had any pride, she told herself, she'd exorcise this attraction that was taking over; she'd get rid of it. How could she love a man who didn't trust her? A man who actually believed she'd betray him for the sake of a news scoop.

Paul said, "I'd appreciate it if you'd give me a blanket."

"What?" Pam asked blankly, mesmerized by the sight of him in a Lincolnesque pose, his gray eyes brooding, his long legs thrust out.

"Despite the fire, it's chilly in here. I plan to stretch out on the couch, so if you could spare a blanket..."

He was going to stay here in her house tonight and there was absolutely nothing she could do about it. Pam absorbed that fact, then shuffled down the hall to her linen closet and ferreted out two thick blankets.

Paul had disappeared when she went back into the living room, and Pam heard water running in the bathroom. She beat a hasty retreat, and a short time later was curled up in bed, thankful for the warmth of her electric blanket.

She would have sworn she wouldn't be able to sleep a wink, knowing that Paul was sprawled out on her living room couch. But within minutes she was dreaming about a dark-haired man whose face she couldn't see clearly.

He kept giving her lie detector tests and making sure that she flunked them.

———

They both had to have breakfast, Pam reasoned. She was hungry, which was not to be wondered at. She'd left Jacob Wirth's yesterday before she'd had lunch, and hadn't bothered to stop for anything to eat on the way back to Bryant Lake.

It would go against her grain to fix something for herself without including Paul, no matter how she felt about his presence. Like it or not, he *was* a guest in her house.

She was flipping pancakes on the grill when Paul came into the kitchen. He looked like he hadn't slept too well. She wondered if he'd had crazy dreams, too.

She fixed him a stack of pancakes and said, "There's butter and syrup on the table."

"You didn't have to go to all this trouble."

"Making pancakes isn't much trouble. The coffee pot's on the table, too."

They ate in silence. Afterward, they shared the cleanup. Paul washed. Pam dried the dishes and cutlery and put them away.

With the last dish stashed in the cupboard, she said, "I'm going up to Cullum's to do some shopping."

"Please wait to go anywhere till after Jerry comes."

Paul spoke quietly, but Pam had no doubt at all that if she attempted to walk out of the house right now he'd stop her.

She tried to work up some outrage over the idea of being held prisoner in her own home, but failed. It was very difficult to remain angry with Paul, especially when he looked so unhappy.

He was living proof that a lot of the time being rich and famous wasn't very much fun.

Paul bridged the strained silence. "Would you like me to read your father's journal to you until Jerry gets here?" he suggested.

Pam hesitated only briefly. "Thanks," she said, "but I don't think I could possibly concentrate on Dad's journal today."

"Pam, I'm sorry." He sounded as though he really meant it.

Pam knew she was too unhinged to take much in the way of apology from him. If he kept looking at her the way he was looking now, she'd melt. Next thing she knew, all the tears she'd been hoarding would come unglued and she'd be in his arms, getting his shoulder sopping wet again.

She closed her eyes tight. How she yearned to be in his arms again, despite everything that had gone down between them.

Her wish came true.

He smelled so good—of musk and maleness and deep pine woods, all combined into an essence that was exclusively his. Pam pressed her cheek against his chest and yielded to the moment. Paul felt strong, warm and wonderful, and for right now just having him hold her was enough.

She wondered how long they might have stood in the middle of the living room, just holding on to each other and not saying anything, if Jerry Bernstein hadn't come knocking on the door.

Chapter Ten

"I drove past your place," Jerry said. "There's no one there."

"That doesn't surprise me," Paul allowed.

"I brought what you wanted."

"Later," Paul said.

Jerry looked from Paul to Pam, then back to Paul again. Pam had the uneasy feeling that she was somehow involved in whatever was going on between the two of them. Then Jerry warned, "You'd both better brace yourself for this."

"What's happened?" Paul asked.

"Angela and a lot of the people involved with the show are on their way up here."

Pam froze, but Paul only queried, "So soon?"

"You were expecting them?"

"Weren't you?"

"What the hell?" Jerry was puzzled. "You haven't been talking to Angela, have you?"

Pam's pulse thumped and her mouth felt dry. Last night, when she was asleep, could Paul have called Angela Santoro? Did he *want* a reunion after all?

Paul said, "No, I haven't been talking to Angela. But I know her. You don't think she'd miss an opportunity like this, do you? I'm sure she's thought of something tremendously dramatic to pull off. And I don't think Attila and his hordes could stop her."

He paused. "When do you think she'll get here?"

"They're driving," Jerry reported unhappily. "A whole damned caravan. My guess is they'll be here by early morning. Sid Brown has booked all the rooms in a place called the Lakeside Inn, and a bunch more at bed-and-breakfasts around here. He had most of his staff working all night."

Jerry added, "And I know what Angela's thought up."

"Well?"

"She's claiming you've had amnesia."

Paul snorted derisively. "Give me a break."

"Angela will use it for all it's worth." Jerry plopped down onto Pam's couch. His plump body sagged. "You might as well know that Angela's in her glory."

Paul chuckled. "I don't doubt that."

"To cap it off, her private eyes found your Jag in her garage. Matter of fact, she was about to go with the suicide story—just like I told you she would—when CBS gave her a call and told her you'd been found alive and well up here in Vermont. She did a quick change of script."

"You've talked to her?"

"No. Actually I tried to phone her late last night, after I saw the first TV bulletin, but by then she wasn't taking any more calls. This morning it was too early to

get to her before I left the city. I talked to Sid Brown's
assistant."

"Lou?"

"That's right."

"What did Lou say?"

Pam sat down across from Jerry and resisted the im-
pulse to clutch her head in her hands. She was devel-
oping a full-scale headache. The interchange between
Paul and Jerry was fast paced, and each sentence was
adding lines to a disaster chart, as far as she was concerned. Even worse, one hard fact emerged that
couldn't be worked around.

Angela Santoro was coming to Bryant Lake. By tonight, Paul would be Jason St. Clair again—like it or
not. There was no way he could avoid a confrontation
with his costar, no matter how he felt about her.

How *did* he feel about her?

Pam watched Paul, and it seemed to her there was a
new, crisp professionalism about him. He was already
pulling away from her.

"What did Lou say?" Jerry repeated Paul's question.

"Lou says Angela has her act together. She's claiming you wanted to get married right away, you were going to talk her into flying down to the islands where
there's no waiting period. Then you could have honey-
mooned at your place in Antigua.

"Angela's saying she was holding out for a Thanksgiving wedding because she felt the two of you owed it
to your fans to include them in. Seems she has this idea
of the ceremony being performed on TV."

Finally, Paul's facade cracked a little. He frowned.
"You can't be serious."

"Believe me, *Angela* is very serious. She's worked out the theory that you were despondent and you went up to her place in Connecticut. You were trying to get her to meet you up there so you could talk to her without anyone else around, but she had commitments in Manhattan she couldn't get away from. She's saying you evidently tripped over something in her living room, because the private eyes found a table overturned and a china lamp smashed."

"I didn't even go in her damned living room."

"She needed to think up a head injury for you to make the amnesia story valid," Jerry pointed out.

Disgusted, Paul said, "Sid would fire any writer who came up with a plot like that. I hope you told Lou we're not going along with this."

Pam began to breathe a little easier.

"Sure I told Lou," Jerry muttered. "But you know Angela. She makes damned good copy. It's lucky you've got some ideas of your own. Otherwise . . ."

Pam caught the warning glance Paul slanted in his agent's direction. Jerry looked every bit as guilty as he probably was.

What were they up to?

Jerry shivered and complained, "Is it always so cold up here?"

"It gets a helluva lot colder." Paul laughed. "Right now I wish we'd have an early blizzard that would block the roads for miles around. That would serve the whole bunch of them right."

"I think Sid would hire dogsleds."

"Sid's coming himself?"

"You better believe it. Lou said this will be Sid's happiest day in a long time. The ratings on the show will soar with this kind of publicity. The sponsors will be purring...."

"I suppose so." Paul brightened. "That's all the more reason why Griffith McQueen can be finished off for once and for all right now. Angela's grief over losing him can be written into the next couple of scripts. Then a new doctor can join the hospital staff."

"I don't know if Angela will buy that."

Paul's smile was enigmatic. "We'll see."

Jerry looked at Pam again, and seemed about to say something. But Paul intervened.

He turned to Pam. "How about putting on some warmer clothes and the two of us getting out for a while?" he suggested. "Maybe we could climb Lyon's Peak."

"The trail will be too muddy," Pam said quickly.

She was glad to be able to latch on to an excuse. The last thing she wanted was a one-on-one outing with Paul. She'd be so tense she'd trip over her tongue and fall over her feet.

"Then let's just get out," he urged.

"What about Jerry?" Pam hedged.

"Jerry can hold the fort here. You'll want to make some phone calls, anyway, won't you, Jerry? It would be a good idea for you to make contact with Bert Cullum up at the general store, too. Bert knows everything that's going on around here. By now, I'm sure he's well aware who I am. But I think he'll be on my side. He might even get a kick out of my having pulled the wool over his eyes a little."

Paul was watching Pam as he spoke. His scrutiny made her uncomfortable. He continued, "Ask Bert to call you as soon as Angela and the rest of them check in at the inn. I guarantee he'll be among the first to know.

Meantime, Pam and I will phone you once in a while from wherever we are, so we'll know what the score is. Pam..."

"Yes?"

"Go put on something warmer, will you? That sweater you're wearing looks pretty thin."

When Pam came back, wearing a thick turtleneck and a padded anorak, Paul was talking to Jerry, his voice so low she couldn't make out what he was saying.

He turned and smiled at her. "That looks warm."

They were in the Trooper driving away from Bryant Lake when she demanded, "Just what is this all about, Paul?"

"What do you mean?"

"Please don't act so innocent. You have something up your sleeve."

"What makes you think that?"

"Your sleeve's bulging."

"You're too sharp, love."

"Look, Paul, whatever happens here once Angela arrives has nothing to do with me. I hope you understand that."

"No," Paul said calmly, "I don't. In my opinion, you're going to have a lot to do with whatever happens."

"Please..." Pam protested wearily.

She felt that silvery glance scan her face. Then Paul said, "It won't be that bad, Pam. Yes, I'm going to involve you. But I think you have that coming, don't you?"

She sighed. "You still think I broke the story about you, don't you?"

Paul waited so long to answer that Pam wondered if maybe he'd become so absorbed in his own thoughts he hadn't heard her. But then he said, "I don't want to get into that now, Pam."

The hurt she'd felt last night had receded a little. Now it came back again, and the pain was worse than ever.

Pam made a decision. She said, "I'd like you to drive me over to Newport, Paul, and let me off there."

"Newport?"

"We went through Newport the other day on our way back from Canada."

"Yes, I know."

"There are some back roads that would be more direct, but they could be pretty bad after so much rain. I think we'd better stick to the paved roads, so if you take the next left..."

Paul pulled over to the side of the road and parked. Then he folded his arms as he faced Pam, and his face was grim.

"I'm not about to take a left anywhere until you tell me why you want me to leave you in Newport," he stated.

"I can get a bus back to Boston from there."

"There's no way I'm going to let you take a bus back to Boston. Unless..." He looked grimmer than ever. "Unless you've decided you're going to marry Alfred," he finished.

Pam wished she was a better liar. She settled for, "This has nothing to do with Alfred."

"Then what does it have to do with?"

"I want to get away, that's all."

"Join the club," Paul said bitterly. "Not that I want to get away any longer. I'm where I want to be. I just want to get rid of all the excess baggage that's been cluttering my life."

He paused. "I need your help if I'm going to do that, Pam."

"My help?" She was genuinely surprised. "How could I possibly help you?"

"I'll tell you in a minute." Paul started the car again. "First, I'd like to put a little more distance between us and Bryant Lake. Suppose we head over toward New Hampshire?"

She shrugged. "It doesn't matter."

"Navigate, will you?"

"Okay, keep heading north. Then hang a right on the next paved road. That'll start us toward North Stratford. Now suppose you answer the question I asked you in the first place."

"What was that?"

"What's this all about?"

Pam studied Paul's profile as she waited for his answer. She'd become used to his being the handsomest man she'd ever seen . . . and now she knew that the way he made her feel went beyond looks.

He touched deep chords in her. He made her aware of feelings, emotions she'd never explored before. Especially since her rescue from the icy lake waters, she'd found that life seemed different, each moment precious. . . .

He said suddenly, "You're wondering what this is all about, and it isn't that easy to tell you, Pam. I think I'm only beginning to appreciate the enormity of the favor I need to ask of you."

"What are you talking about?"

"I wish there was a place where we could be alone and talk things out." He sounded distracted. "Riding around back roads doesn't do it for me."

"You sound like this is a TV show, Paul. It isn't."

Anger flashed in his eyes. "You think I don't know that?" Then he sighed. "Hear me out, will you?"

"I'm listening."

"Pam—will you trust me for the next twenty-four hours?"

She stared at him. "That's pretty crazy. You're asking someone whom you don't trust at all to trust you?"

"That's something I guess we'll have to talk about before I go any further." The confession came slowly. "I know you didn't break that story, Pam."

Stunned, she asked, "Do you know who did?"

"No. But my gut feeling is that you wouldn't do that to me."

"Last night..." Pam began.

Paul cut her off. "Yes, I know how I came across last night. Will you try to understand how angry and frustrated I was? You became my scapegoat, and I regret that very much."

He went on, "You see...for the past three years, ever since I first came up here to Vermont, I've been thinking more and more about something that's very important to me. Lately, I was beginning to make plans for a future, a terrific future. It was like seeing that light at the end of the tunnel. My life was starting to swing into focus. Then ... this happened.

"Now... well, now everything is on hold till I clear up the situation with Angela and Sid. I'm hoping to make them see it my way. They know as well as I do how fickle the public is. Once Griffith McQueen fades from the scene people will soon forget about him. That means they'll also forget about Jason St. Clair. Then I'll be free to be myself—for the rest of my life."

There was an odd note in Paul's voice as he added, "But that's not going to happen without your help, Pam."

She sighed. "You're not making sense, Paul."

"Oh, but I am, sweetheart."

Pam watched Paul take a hand off the steering wheel, then fish around in the pocket of his dark green parka.

"Take this, will you?" he asked, and handed her a small paper bag.

She felt a solid square lump inside the bag and looked at him questioningly.

"Please," he said. "Open it."

Pam pulled a small square box out of the bag. The box was covered in blue velvet, and after a quick glance at it she dropped it as if it were a hot coal.

Her mind was racing. This was a jeweler's box, the kind of box a ring came in.

Paul urged, "Keep going, will you?"

"Paul..."

"Pam...just open the damned thing, will you?"

Pam stared at the box. Any illusions she might have had were quickly being dispelled.

A man on the verge of a proposal didn't speak the way Paul had.

She saw that he was clutching the steering wheel so tightly that his knuckles were white.

"Go on!" he commanded.

Pam fought an urge to open the window and toss the box out among the clumps of wild blue asters that grew alongside the road. Instead, she opened it...and found herself gazing at the most beautiful ring she'd ever seen.

The diamond was square cut—large, but not so large as to be ostentatious. The ring was set in platinum, the center stone flanked on either side by four small diamonds. With it was a platinum wedding band, also with diamonds.

"Put them on, will you?"

Pam could hear the tension crackle in Paul's voice. She shook her head. "No."

"Pam, for God's sake, put them on. It's important to know if they fit right. I tried to tell Jerry—"

"This is what Jerry brought you?"

"Yes. Look . . . I'm sorry, I'm sorry. I'm making the worst possible mess out of everything. Let me explain. All I'm asking is that you wear those rings tonight when we go to the inn to meet Angela and the others."

"When *we* go to the inn?"

"Yes."

"Why would I go to the inn with you?"

"Because I want Angela to think we're married."

"It will work," Paul went on, when Pam didn't answer him. "I'll tell Angela we got married three years ago, just before I bought my cottage at Bryant Lake. You've had your family cottage for years—I'll say I bought a place near you so we could meet up here without raising anyone's suspicions. That'll seem logical enough. If Bert Cullum, for instance, knew you had a man living in your place with you, sooner or later explanations would have to be made. But no one would question two Martins having places along the lake. We could rendezvous whenever we wanted to without arousing any special attention."

Pam shook her head. "I don't believe you. You're making this sound like fact instead of fiction."

"It'll have to sound like fact if Angela's going to buy it."

"I can't believe I'm hearing this. What do you take me for? You're asking me to pretend to be your *wife?*"

Her voice rose. "Well, let me tell you right now, there's no way I'm going to lie like that for you."

Again, Paul pulled to the side of the road. Then he forced Pam to meet his eyes as he said, "At the worst, we'd be telling a white lie. Actually, it would be an act of kindness. I don't want to hurt Angela. When I first went on the show with her—"

"I don't want to hear about when you first went on the show with Angela."

Paul waited a minute. Then he said, "I think there's something you should know before we go any further. I've never had a relationship with Angela Santoro—of any kind. She's fabricated these stories of a romance between us out of . . . well, I guess I have to call it desperation.

"When I was first on the show with her, though, she was kind to me. She was already an established star, remember. I was a newcomer—a pretty green newcomer. As it happened, Griffith McQueen, M.D. took off, and it's been harder and harder for her to keep up. That's why so much hype has been built up about the two of us. If the viewing audience thinks there's something going on between us, it keeps them interested in Angela as well as me.

"I went along with that. I didn't give a damn, to tell you the truth. There was no reason to undercut her. Frankly, I felt it would have been needlessly cruel. There was no one else in my life. No one her stories could affect.

"I even sloughed it off when she started to get specific with this plan for a Thanksgiving wedding," Paul admitted. "It goes without saying nothing like that would have ever happened. I figured she could think of a way out that would save face and even make her look good. In fact, when Jerry came up with that scenario about her pretending I'd disappeared because she'd rejected me, it seemed like a pretty viable solution. I would have gone along with that.

"Angela is a lot older than she looks, Pam. She's already had a couple of face-lifts. She's a reasonably good actress, but her stock in trade has been playing sexy roles. Where that's concerned her time is limited, and she knows it. So she's fighting like a tigress for what she's got. She's going to hang on with every ounce of strength in her—and she's a pretty strong woman. But the time has come when this whole thing has to stop. If we follow my idea of killing McQueen, Angela can have a field day awhile longer. The fans will eat it all up. So I'm not doing anything to hurt her."

Pam had heard enough. She put the blue plush box into the paper bag and thrust the bag at Paul.

"Take this," she commanded.

He pushed the bag away. "Please," he said, "hear me out. What I'm asking of you wouldn't go beyond five people—you, Jerry, Angela, Sid and me. When we get to the Lakeside Inn, I'll tell Angela I need to speak to her alone. Then I'll tell her the story I just told you. At that point, I'll ask you to join us. She'll meet you, she'll see the rings. After that, I'll go along with her amnesia story or any other damned thing that'll get me off the hook. And I'll be free, so..."

Pam glared at him. "No!"

To her surprise, Paul shrugged.

"All right." He sounded calm, but his face paled.

He glanced at his watch. "I'll find a phone in the next town we come to and I'll call Jerry," he said. "Then we can turn back."

There was a finality in his tone. They were once again worlds apart.

He remained remote, a stranger to her, as he left her to make his phone call, and then came back to the car to ask, "Would you like to stop for coffee or anything?"

Why did she feel so *small* about all of this? She said stiffly, "No thanks."

The drive back to Bryant Lake seemed interminable. About the time they reached the turnoff that led to Lost Lake, it began to rain again.

Paul pulled up along the road in front of Pam's cottage and said, "I'll go on up to my place. Tell Jerry to come along, will you?"

He drove off without waiting for her answer.

Despite the rain, Pam stood at the side of the road and stared after the red Trooper until Paul rounded the bend and she couldn't see the car anymore.

What he'd asked of her was preposterous.

So why did she feel as though she'd failed him?

Chapter Eleven

"Where did he go?" Jerry asked.

"To his place," Pam said. "He wants you to go over there."

Jerry's eyes were round, and very pale blue. They looked worried and unhappy. Pam sensed he had a lot of questions, but was trying to be discreet.

She said dully, "He asked me, Jerry."

Jerry nodded. "I guessed that, Pamela. I'm also guessing you turned him down."

"Yes."

"If you don't mind...was this for real or was it fake?"

Surprised, she said, "Fake, naturally. What else?"

"I didn't know which way it might go."

Pam stared at Jerry. "All Paul wanted was a wife for maybe an hour—at the most."

She hadn't meant to put it that way, hadn't meant to let on to her sadness and bitterness.

Jerry said, "Maybe."

"There's no cause for doubt, Jerry."

"This is a bad time," Jerry said. "I don't envy Jace. He could do without this. Angela's going to pull out all the stops."

"I get the impression you think I've made it harder for him."

Those round, light blue eyes could be disconcerting. "You want the truth?"

She nodded.

"All right. Yes, I think you've made it harder for him. But that's not your problem. You had to do what you felt was right for you."

Pam studied a spot on the living room rug. She deliberated, then asked, "Jerry, do you drink sherry?"

He smiled. "Sure. Why not?"

Minutes later, Pam was sitting at her kitchen table, sharing what was left of her bottle of sherry with one of New York's sharpest theatrical agents. She was also discovering that he was as unhinged over Paul as she was.

"I'm crazy about that guy, Pamela," Jerry confessed. "Okay, so I'll be schmaltzy and say it—he's like a son to me. Now I could kick myself, because I thought I was doing what was best for him. I admit it, I was thinking money, I was thinking of the long run. I was thinking, this doesn't make sense, a guy right at the top of his career walking out."

Jerry sighed. "I was wrong. Jace doesn't need money, he's had it up to his neck with the show. Now's the time for him to do his own thing. I should have seen that. He wanted out. I should have told Sid Brown, no deal. All right, at one point I *told* Sid no deal, and what did Sid do? Sid offered a pay jump I couldn't believe. If I'd *asked* for it—"

"Jerry," Pam said softly, "stop torturing yourself. You stalled a little, you held things up for Paul, maybe, but that's not so terrible. He hasn't lost that much time."

"Paul." Jerry smiled wryly. "I guess I'll have to get used to that. It's going to take some doing. He was Paul when I first knew him, but that goes pretty far back."

"What was he like when you first met him, Jerry?"

"Ten years ago," Jerry said. "What was he like? He had a Southern accent that was thick as butter."

"He said it took a lot of work to get rid of it."

Jerry's eyebrows rose. "He told you about that?"

"Yes. He told me about...about where he came from."

"Then you're the first. The first woman, anyway. And we'd known each other quite awhile before I got his story out of him."

He studied her face. "Don't be too quick about making up your mind about him, Pamela."

Jerry left abruptly after that, leaving Pam to wonder exactly what he had meant.

Her day was shot. There was no point in going near her father's journals—she couldn't read, she couldn't concentrate. It was too cold to go swimming, and after the other day she wasn't geared up to the idea of swimming alone, anyway. She thought about taking a walk, but she had a choice of the road or the lakefront. Either route would take her past Paul's cottage, and she didn't want to go near his place.

The afternoon wore on. Finally, toward six, Pam drove up to Cullum's store because she was out of both coffee and milk. Bert usually stayed open till at least six on Saturdays, and she doubted today would be an exception. The general store was the local gathering place, and there was going to be more excitement in Bryant Lake tonight than there'd been for a long, long time.

Bert verified that when he beamed as he greeted her and said, "Things haven't been hopping like this around here since that scientist from Albany thought he saw one of the Loch Ness monster's cousins out in the lake a few years back."

He frowned. "You look kind of peaked, Pam."

"I've felt better," Pam admitted. Had she ever!

The store was a beehive of activity, but not because people were shopping. They were coming and going or standing around in little clumps, the conversation a steady stream of conjecture spiced with supposed news bulletins.

"I think I just saw her car pull up in front of the inn," a gray-haired woman announced.

"Naw," a man who was one of Bert's regulars contradicted, "that was another one of them reporting teams from New York. You know what?"

There was an expectant pause.

"We got to get up a committee and talk to the people who run the cable company over in Newport. It's time to see what they can do about bringing in decent TV around here."

"I'll serve," two people said simultaneously.

Bert, who'd been standing behind the counter, emerged and drew Pam over to a corner back of the big standing refrigerator unit.

"Henry Beeman fingered him," he said.

Pam stared at Bert. "What?"

"Henry Beeman figured out that Paul Martin was really Jason St. Clair, the big TV star."

"Henry Beeman?"

Bert nodded. "Henry's wife, Clara—maybe you know her?"

Pam shook her head.

"Clara's got a sister who lives down in Florida. They go down winters on Henry's vacation. Clara's sister's hooked on that show Jason St. Clair's on and she got Clara hooked on it. Henry says the two of them made him watch it every day, too, and if you ask me I think he liked it.

"He'd seen Martin—guess I should call him St. Clair—in here, and he says there was something sort of familiar about him but he didn't think too much of it. Then he saw him jogging along the lake road a couple of times. He didn't have on those glasses he usually wears and Henry said all of a sudden it hit him.

"Henry told Clara, and Clara called up her sister in Florida and she said it was all over the news down there that St. Clair had disappeared and that woman on the show with him—the one who's on her way up here—was saying she thought he committed suicide because he was crazy in love with her. Or else maybe somebody's jealous husband or boyfriend murdered him...."

"Oh my God!" Pam muttered.

"Pam," Bert called, "a guy named Bernstein who says he's St. Clair's agent called me up and asked me if I'd tell him as soon as the people from the show check in at the inn. The number he gave me to call back was your phone number."

Pam didn't say anything.

"Also," Bert said, "Henry's been saying he thinks he got the mail for the two of you mixed up. Two P. Martins, he says. How was he supposed to know? But my guess is you straightened out the mail yourselves, didn't you?''

"Yes," Pam admitted.

"Pam, some people are saying there's been something going on all along between you and St. Clair—he even used your name when he bought his place up here."

Pam stared at Bert.

Unexpectedly, Bert grinned. "I think it's great," he said. "I got a lot of questions, I admit. Like why you waited so long to join him up here. Far as I know, he's been coming for the past three years on his own."

Bert's grin widened. "I can't think you could have been coming up here without my knowing it."

"Bert . . ." Pam began.

"Look, Pam, that day he came in and said you were blocking his car, and you asked about him—I swear I could feel the sparks flying between the two of you. I told you then he's a nice guy. That's the truth, whether he's a big TV star or not. He's a *damned* nice guy, Pam, and I'm all for it."

Pam couldn't answer.

"Bert!"

The tall thin blonde now standing in the front door was waving frantically. She said in a rush, "There's no doubt about it. A block-long gray limo just pulled up in front of the inn and . . . and, yes, she's getting out. . . .''

"The hell you say," Bert exclaimed, abandoned Pam and went to join the crowd gathering outside his store.

Pam leaned against Bert's scarred wooden counter and desperately tried to regroup.

Bert had taken a few quantum leaps in his assessment of the situation between Paul and herself. And, knowing Bert as she did, she had no doubt that he'd already shared his opinion with a fair number of his customers.

There was nothing malicious about Bert. He was just a lovable old gossip who enjoyed people and liked to see them happy. But right now she could have strangled him.

She heard the excited voices, the clamor, and she'd never felt more alone. If she'd never met Paul, maybe she'd be out there with the rest of them, sharing in the event and getting some fun out of it.

As it was...

Pam wandered to the back of Bert Cullum's store, made her way through the storage area and out a rear door. She reclaimed her car and was glad she'd parked it out back instead of along the street—which had become her usual custom since that first encounter with Paul.

She drove away from the store, away from the inn, away from the little town, struck out on the lake road and bypassed her cottage.

She slowed as she reached Paul's place, then made a final decision and put on her brakes.

The rental car Jerry used was gone, but the Isuzu Trooper was still there. There was a dim light on in the living room, otherwise the house was in darkness.

Pam got out of the car slowly, still thinking, still deliberating, still wanting to be sure about what she was going to do next.

Was Paul inside?

She hoped not.

She hoped so.

He wasn't.

Pam pounded on the front door till she was sure of that. Then she walked around the house toward his back porch.

She'd thought to bring her flashlight with her. The beam shone on the place where she'd found the *Calvatia*—years ago, centuries ago, aeons ago...or so it seemed.

There should be a monument on the spot.

She was remembering that Paul had gotten into her house last night via her back door. He'd been somewhat chiding when he'd said she always locked her front door and then went and left her kitchen door open.

Could he be guilty of the same thing?

He was.

Pam turned the doorknob cautiously. The door creaked a little as it opened.

She giggled nervously, then more than half expected to hear Paul's voice emerge from the darkness, just as it had last night in her house. But there was only silence.

Paul and Jerry had gone to the Lakeside Inn. That seemed pretty obvious. Right now, Paul and Angela Santoro were probably meeting. TV cameras would be filming the scene, the print media would be taking still photographs, reporters would be firing questions....

Pam switched on a lamp, verified that the living room was empty, went through the rest of the house and satisfied herself that she was alone.

Then she paused.

She could use a little guidance from a professional burglar, she thought whimsically. As it was, she was going to have to start from scratch—and hope she could find what she was looking for.

* * *

There was no such thing as a parking space anywhere near the Lakeside Inn. Pam drove back to the spot she'd vacated earlier behind Cullum's store, left the car, then cut through a couple of lots and walked along Main Street the rest of the way.

The lobby of the inn was a madhouse. Some heads turned in Pam's direction as she walked in, but no one paid any real attention to her.

There was value to anonymity, she was discovering. She didn't want to say anything to anyone until she accomplished her objective. But in order to do *that,* she had to find Jerry.

She saw some cameras flashing, and followed a hunch. Jerry, surrounded by reporters, was fielding questions.

Pam stood on tiptoe, caught his eye and nodded. Then she turned and walked out of the inn and sauntered along Main Street.

The curb was lined with stretch limos, vans, pickups and a variety of cars. There were people clustered around, and down the street there was still a crowd gathered out in front of Cullum's store. The sodium vapor lights the town highway department had installed a few years back cast a yellow light over everything. Bryant Lake looked like a set for a thirties movie, Pam thought.

She walked slowly. In a few minutes, Jerry caught up with her.

He was slightly out of breath. "I'm not used to this kind of exercise," he complained. "You wanted me, Pamela?"

She nodded, "Yes."

"So?" Jerry queried.

"I have to see him, Jerry. Right now."

"We'll be stampeded if the reporters spot us together, Pamela. It won't take them thirty seconds to get the message something's up."

Jerry was just about her height. Their eyes met on an equal level.

"Something is up, isn't it?" he asked her.

"I . . . I think so."

He didn't pursue the issue, for which Pam was grateful. She didn't want to stop to think, she didn't want to stop to talk. If she did either, she could so easily lose her nerve.

She said, "I got out of Cullum's earlier by a back door. There have to be some back ways out of the inn."

"You know the place better than I do."

"Mmm . . . I've had dinner here many times. There's a long porch that looks out over the lake. They have little round tables out there, and serve drinks there in the summer, and maybe lunch. Dinner—in the dining room—is more formal.

"There are a couple of doors that went from the porch into the dining room. Then a door leads into a room that could be used as a private dining room or for meetings . . . I think."

"That must be the room Angela and Sid are holed up in with Jace . . . I mean Paul," Jerry said. "I'm supposed to join them. I had to stop to talk to the press first."

He mused, "Maybe they'll have security guards on the porch, but it's okay if they do. I've got identification. It's worth a try, Pamela."

It was dark and shady around the back of the inn. A grassy slope led down to the lake, and the ground was still squishy from the recent rain. Pam had forgotten her flashlight this time, and she wished she'd brought it. She also wished she'd worn flats. She had on her city shoes, and the heels were sticking in the mud.

Jerry nearly fell over a stony outcropping and swore. "Take me out of Manhattan and I'm in constant danger," he muttered.

Pam chuckled, glad of anything to lighten up the situation. "You're doing fine, Jerry," she assured him.

No one challenged them as they started up the steps. The formal dining room was open only for the season and was now dark. But lights blazed from the other room, and the drapes were drawn back from the huge picture window that looked out toward the water.

Jerry found the right door, tried the knob and again he swore. "The damned thing's locked."

Pam peered through the window. She saw three people on the far side of the room: Paul, a big, beefy man with carrot-red hair, and...Angela Santoro.

Paul's costar was dressed in vivid, dramatic red, the perfect foil for her dark coloring. She was beautiful, Pam thought. From here, anyway, she looked even more beautiful than she did on television.

Pam's heart started to ache.

Then she focused on Paul. He was wearing black slacks and a black crew knit sweater. He looked... fantastic. Different, somehow.

He wasn't wearing his glasses.

"Oh, God," Pam moaned, "he'll never see us."

At her side, Jerry asked, "What do you mean?"

"Paul. I want to try to attract his attention but he can't see clearly from that distance without his glasses."

"My guess is he has his contacts on, Pamela."

"I hope you're right."

Pam tried tapping on the window. The sound was much too feeble to be heard. Paul appeared to be having a heated dialogue with the redheaded man....

Pam pulled off one of her city shoes, raised the heel, and banged it on the window.

She didn't care if she broke the glass.

She banged again. And suddenly, Paul was looking right at her.

He broke away from the redheaded man and strode across the room, and Pam felt sure that if he hadn't been able to open the door he'd have broken the lock.

He stood in the doorway. "Pam?" he queried uncertainly. His voice sounded strange and hollow.

"Hello, darling," Pam said—loud enough so she hoped her words would carry across the room.

Paul looked at her as if she'd lost her mind. Then she held out her hand.

The square-cut diamond blazed on her ring finger. Below it, the diamond-and-platinum wedding band sparkled.

Paul stared at her incredulously and didn't move. It was Jerry who gave her a slight shove, pushing her across the threshold.

Finally, Paul took the clue. He clasped Pam's arm, led her forward, and said, "Angela, Sid, I want you to meet my wife."

The silence that followed was deafening.

Never in her life had Pam faced the kind of hostility she was seeing. Venomous was the only way to describe Angela Santoro.

The actress *was* beautiful. But she looked a lot older in person than she did on TV. Paul was right. Angela's days were numbered, when it came to playing romantic leads.

Despite the venom, Pam felt a pang of sympathy for her. It must be terrible to have to be so desperate.

"This is a sorry joke, Jason," Angela said.

Paul shook his head. "It's no joke, Angela. Pam and I have been married over three years. That's why I bought my place here. Pam inherited a cottage on the lake from her father. We thought it would be best if I maintained a house here, too, to lessen the chance of gossip. Pam agreed we shouldn't announce our marriage until I was ready to leave the show.

"After all," Paul concluded, "Griffith McQueen had to remain the ultimate bachelor, wouldn't you say?"

"I say I don't believe you," Angela told him. "You're a lousy actor, Paul. You always have been. I don't know why you're doing this, but you're using this woman as a…a ploy. I would think you could be more original."

Tally one for Angela.

Pam waited to see what Paul was going to offer in the way of rebuttal. He didn't speak. He merely took hold of her left hand, held it out, and let Angela see the gorgeous rings sparkling on her finger.

Angela flinched.

"I didn't want to do it like this," Paul said huskily. "Believe me."

Was he talking to Angela or to her? Pam wondered.

"I wanted things to be different," he went on, and no one could have sounded more sincere.

Pam listened, and decided that Paul was a better actor than either he or Angela thought he was.

"Pam...as I'm sure you already know, this is Angela Santoro. And this is Sid Brown."

She nodded.

"I'm not going back to the show," Paul said. "I'm not going to sign a new contract. Jerry has accepted that. Now, Angela, Sid, I'm asking you to accept it, too. If you think I ever made any verbal agreements with you, Sid, you're mistaken. All I can say is, you weren't hearing what I really was saying. Now..."

Paul smiled slowly. "I think you should ditch me, Angela."

She stared at him. "What?"

"*When Tomorrow Comes* is a great show. There's no reason why it should fold because Griffith meets an untimely death while he's saving lives in Central America. There are plenty of photogenic guys out there who are much better actors than I am. One of them, I'm sure, would give his eyeteeth for the chance to join the medical staff at Anderson-Gorman General Hospital.

"But," Paul finished succinctly, "there is only one Angela Santoro."

Pam couldn't look at him.

"As for Jason St. Clair," Paul said, "I'll go along with whatever will be best for the show, Angela. If you think the fans will buy the amnesia story, fine. We can say I went up to your place, hoping you'd meet me there so I could talk you into eloping with me. I tripped over a table in your living room and hit my head on the corner of your baby grand as I fell down. When I came to, I didn't know where I was.

"I woke up in a motel room in Burlington, Vermont. I felt very mixed-up, very shaky. I needed to be alone. I rented a car and came to the hideaway cottage I bought a while back. That would do for starters, don't you think?"

Pam didn't even hear Angela's answer. Her knees felt as though they belonged to someone else, her hands were clammy. The stress was getting to her.

She'd never been cut out to be a liar.

Someone grabbed her arm. Jerry.

"I'll see Pam home, then I'll come back," he said. "I think Pam and I can slip out the same way we got in. Why don't you work out a statement for the press that will be agreeable to everyone."

Jerry tugged Pam's arm, and she knew she had to move. But her legs were like wooden sticks.

She heard Angela Santoro say, "Is your *wife* willing to go along with this, Jason?"

Pam didn't wait for Paul to answer.

"I'm willing to do whatever's best, Miss Santoro," she said.

That was true enough. Right now all she wanted was to get out in the fresh air.

But there was to be another step.

Paul bent over and kissed her squarely on the lips. There was no passion in the kiss. It was cool and...efficient. Pam felt as if they'd just signed a business contract. She also felt a little sick.

Once outside, she suddenly sat down on the bottom porch step and said, "Sorry, Jerry. I'll pull it together in a minute, but right now I'm a little bit dizzy."

Jerry sat down next to her. "Take your time. The media's concentrating on what's going on inside, and I'll bet you Sid has already told them there'll be a statement and maybe interviews as well in a little while.

"You were great," Jerry told her. "Really great." He brightened. "Ever think about going into show business?"

Pam started to laugh. And she kept on laughing and laughing until, finally, she began to cry.

Chapter Twelve

The coffee canister in the kitchen was empty. There was no milk in the fridge. There were a couple of dry crusts of bread in a plastic bag on the counter.

Pam had completely forgotten about mundane details like grocery shopping once she'd walked into Bert Cullum's store yesterday. Bert had waylaid her . . . and looking back now she could see that had been the turning point.

From then on, she'd let herself be swept along on a strange tide that had little to do with logic.

Would she do things differently if she could set back the clock twelve hours? As she brewed a cup of tea and took it back to the living room, where she'd built a fire, Pam admitted to herself that in all honesty she didn't know. She did know she wished Paul hadn't kissed her at the last moment. He'd given her a stage kiss, closed lips, dry as paper. He'd been performing. He'd made her feel as though she was a partner in a cold-blooded business agreement.

The experience had been . . . humiliating.

Jerry had tried to soothe her as he'd walked her back to her car. Fortunately, no one had noticed them.

Jerry had kept saying that everything was going to work out. He was a nice man, but Pam had no illusions about things working out where she and Paul were concerned. Paul, she was remembering, had wanted freedom.

Well . . . now he had it. He could go his way alone, unencumbered by either people or a career.

Pam's spirits were close to rock bottom when she heard someone pounding on the back door.

Paul?

She wasn't ready to confront him yet. Later, she'd have to return his rings. But right now . . .

The pounding continued.

Maybe it was Jerry. Maybe Paul had sent Jerry over to pick up the rings.

On the other hand, maybe it was someone from the media who'd been alerted by Bert Cullum to her role in last night's drama.

Fortunately, she hadn't seen any familiar faces from the Boston press corps at Lakeside Inn. But that didn't mean she might not later have been identified and . . .

Pam heard Paul yell, "You might as well open up, or I'll break the damned thing down."

Pam, trying to muster up anger and defiance with every move, slowly crossed the room and opened the door.

Paul scowled down at her, and she had to admit he'd never seemed less charismatic. He was wearing jeans and a bright red sweater, but he looked terrible. There were dark circles under his eyes that even his glasses couldn't camouflage. He needed a shave; his hair was tousled.

He said abruptly, "For once, you locked your back door."

She nodded.

"We have to talk, Pam."

Pam hadn't gotten dressed yet. Her long pink flannel robe was so old, most of the color was washed out of it, but it was soft and comfortable and she couldn't bear to throw it away. Her fuzzy slippers were well past their prime. She'd twisted her hair into a makeshift knot on top of her head that left wisps falling in all directions. Her eyelids were still puffy.

She said, "Maybe we can talk later. Not now. I'm going back to bed for a while."

Paul shook his head. "Now." He added lightly, "I didn't sleep any better than you did"

"Where's Jerry?"

"Asleep," Paul said. "I came back to the house after we got through with the press interviews but Jerry was tied up with Sid after that, hashing things out. Pam—"

"Did everything work out as you wanted it to?"

"No."

"You mean . . . you'll have to sign another contract?"

"No, I'm not signing another contract. Sid backed down. Griffith McQueen, M.D. will soon be injured by a band of guerrillas, and he will die from his wounds. Angela will mourn for a while, and she looks great in black. Everyone's very happy."

"Happy?"

"Yes. Jerry came up with a great idea. Sid's going to launch a nationwide contest to select a guy to replace Griffith on the staff at Anderson-Gorman General Hospital. They've even picked his name. Grant Bartholomew, M.D.

"Angela will select the six men she considers the most devastating from the contestant field. Then, the viewers will be asked to vote. The publicity will be fantastic. The ratings will soar. The sponsors will go crazy with joy. That's why everyone's happy."

"Except you?"

"That's right," Paul agreed. "Except me. Look, Pam, do I have to stand out here all day or may I come in? It's cold out here."

Pam hesitated. Then she said none too graciously, "I suppose you might as well come in."

She'd get the rings and return them to him now, she decided. They were valuable. Even though there was no such thing as burglary in Bryant Lake, she didn't want to take chances with someone else's property. And since she wasn't going to be around here much longer . . .

Paul stalked past her.

He went over to the fireplace and stood close to it, rubbing his hands together. Watching him, Pam admitted, "I'm puzzled. What happened? Did you change your mind after it was too late?"

He swung around. "What are you talking about?"

"I'm talking about your leaving the show. Evidently you wish you'd listened to Jerry."

"What makes you think that?"

"Well . . . you said you're not pleased. . . ."

"I didn't say I'm not pleased. You asked me if everything worked out the way I wanted it to, and I said no." He looked around. "Got any coffee?"

"No, I ran out."

"Let's go up to Bert's. He'll have the pot on." Paul thought about that. "Damn, it's Sunday. Bert won't be open."

Pam was bewildered. "Are you saying you'd go up to Bert's if he were open?"

Paul frowned again. "Sure. Why wouldn't I?"

"People are going to recognize you from now on," she warned. "Those glasses aren't a good enough camouflage. Even when you haven't shaved..."

He rubbed his chin. "I didn't want to stop to shave. But, to answer your question—I know people will recognize me. That's something I'll have to accept for a while. I'll probably have to smile, sign a few autographs...."

"I thought..."

"Pam, I've always known that sooner or later I'd be found out, even here in Bryant Lake. It's been great being incognito around here for the past three years... but being found out now doesn't make all that much difference. Fans have short memories. Once Grant Bartholomew's discovered and gets going, I'll be well on my way to being home free."

He shrugged. "For a while people will recognize me, but I can handle that because I know it isn't going to last forever. After a time, someone may wrinkle his brow now and then and say 'Jeez, that guy looks familiar. Wonder where I've seen him before?' But, especially here in Vermont, I'll be allowed to live in peace and lead my own life. That's what I like about the people up here. They're individualists. They like their privacy respected, and they respect the privacy of others."

He smiled wryly. "End of speech," he announced. "Now..."

"Paul..."

"I have this feeling I'm keeping you from something."

"I—I'd started to pack," she admitted. "I stopped to make some coffee but I didn't have any coffee so I made a cup of tea and I..."

"Why are you packing?"

"I'm going away for a while."

"Where?"

Pam sighed. "I don't know."

"You're going away but you don't know where you're going." Paul folded his arms and gave her a long, level look. "Tell me if I've jumped to the correct conclusion. You've decided Bryant Lake's not big enough for both of us, right?"

"Paul, please..."

"Right?"

"Perhaps."

"By any chance were you going to leave without bothering to say goodbye?"

"No," she said quickly. "Because..."

She paused, then added, "Wait a minute."

Pam started for the bedroom, but Paul didn't wait. He followed her.

She was so nervous her hands were shaking as she took the brown paper bag from her top dresser drawer and held it out to him.

"I wanted to be sure to return these," she said.

Paul didn't answer her. But she saw that every trace of expression had been wiped off his face. His eyes traveled to the open suitcase on her bed. She'd tossed some lingerie into the suitcase, then paused to make the tea while trying to decide what to pack next.

Before she picked out the kind of clothes to take with her, she needed to know where she was going.

"You're serious about this, aren't you?" Paul gestured toward the suitcase. "You're actually going to take off."

"Just for a little while."

"And your only reason is to get away from me?"

"Paul, I—"

"Do you really want to get away from me as much as that, Pam?"

"It isn't a question of wanting to get away from you. I need to get away from you till I can . . ."

"Till you can what?"

"Put—put myself together."

"I see. Once you've put yourself together, what are you going to do?"

She stared at him helplessly. "I don't know. That's what I have to think about. I—I guess I'll come back and close up the cottage. I have an apartment in Boston. I don't know if I'll go back there or try to find someplace else where . . . where I can get in the right frame of mind to work on the book."

"What about Alfred? Have you made up your mind about him?"

"Alfred?" Pam echoed weakly. She went over to the bed, pushed the suitcase back and sat down on the edge of the mattress. "Alfred has nothing to do with—with anything I do from now on. I saw him Friday and I told him I can't marry him."

"*That's* why you went to Boston?"

"Yes."

"Why the hell didn't you tell me so?"

Paul snapped the suitcase closed, put it on the floor and sat down next to Pam.

She stiffened, knowing she was going to have to keep very tight control or she'd be apt to make a fool of herself. She was an intelligent, reasoning woman, she reminded herself. It was ridiculous that this man should be able to push up her pulse rate and make pale pink moths flutter around inside her . . . just because he was so close she fancied she could feel his body heat.

"I need to hear something from you," Paul said.

"What?"

"What made you change your mind last night?"

"Change my mind?"

"Why did you show up at the inn with those rings on your finger?"

"I talked to Jerry . . . and I got the rings from your place and . . ."

"You're telling me Jerry persuaded you to do that?"

"No." Pam clasped her hands in her lap and stared down at her fingers. "Jerry didn't know I was going to do it. I went to the inn on my own and found him in the lobby talking to some reporters."

"All right. If you acted on your own, what did talking to Jerry have to do with it?"

"Jerry . . . I think . . . knows you a lot better than most people do."

"I don't deny that. But what does Jerry's knowing me have to do with you?"

"He cares a lot about you."

"I also care a lot about him. You still haven't answered my question, Pam."

Pam heard the urgency in Paul's voice, and suddenly she knew that a great deal hinged on what she said next.

The pink moths disappeared, her pulse rate actually steadied, and for this moment, anyway, Pam was in control as she said again, "Jerry cares a lot about you. And..."

She drew a deep breath. "And so do I," she concluded.

Paul took off his glasses and, elbows on his knees, propped his head between his hands. He was still, everything in the room was so still, that the sound of the clock clicking on the dresser sounded disproportionately loud.

Pam looked at Paul and battled the temptation to plunge her fingers into his thick, dark hair. She held her breath as she waited for a response from him. Then, when there was none, she murmured unsteadily, "Paul?"

His voice was muffled. "You do know how to scare the hell out of a person."

"What are you saying?"

He raised his head and looked at her, his face still strained, the silvery eyes—without the glasses—showing his torment.

"I was afraid I'd made such mess of everything I'd completely blown it with you. And God, I love you so much."

His words echoed in Pam's mind, found their way into her heart, and the explosion of joy was like a shower of golden stars lighting up her life.

Her sight was blinded by tears as she reached for Paul. They rocked in each other's arms. Then their lips met, and fire mixed with rare tenderness in their kiss.

They clung. Then, after a while, Paul drew Pam down on the bed beside him, pillowed his head on her pillow and tugged her close to his side, keeping his arm around her.

"When you walked in that room last night," he said huskily, "I couldn't believe what was happening."

"I know. You looked disbelieving enough when you opened the door for Jerry and me...but you also looked at me as if I were a stranger. And that kiss..."

"Sweetheart, if I hadn't held back the way I did, we'd still be there. Talk about *acting*, talk about self-control...."

"You fooled me," Pam admitted ruefully.

"I was afraid of that. But...I was also so damned ashamed."

"Ashamed?"

He nodded. "I knew I never should have asked anything like that of you. And when you actually showed up...I thought I'd cheapened something that was meant to be beautiful. That's why I said I'd never intended to have it happen like that. That I wished I'd done things differently. I felt...terrible. Because I knew what you were going through. I also knew, too late, that I should have done what I wanted to do in the first place. I should have asked you to marry me the way a man proposes to the woman he loves. If I hadn't thought Alfred was still loitering somewhere backstage..."

Pam smiled. "You're jealous of Alfred."

"I've been jealous as hell of Alfred," Paul growled. "Last night," he went on, "Jerry had to drive me home, because I'd left the Trooper at my place. Then he went back to the inn to meet with the others. Meanwhile, when we came by your house, there were no lights on. I told Jerry I wanted to stop, anyway. He advised against it. He said you'd been pretty upset. He thought it might be better if I gave you the night to cool down a little."

"Jerry was right. I wasn't ready to talk to anyone, let alone reason with them."

"Well...maybe I rushed in too fast this morning, but I couldn't wait any longer. I couldn't sleep a wink. I was pacing the floor when Jerry finally got back from the inn last night. We talked for a long time. He doesn't hold what's happened against me, thank God."

"Of course he doesn't," Pam said. "He told me he knew he was wrong. He said he should have done what you wanted from the beginning."

"He was thinking of me. I can appreciate the fact that it was hard for anyone to believe I really wanted out—even someone who knows me as well as Jerry does. He thought it was just temporary burnout. He wanted to protect my interests."

Paul said slowly, "Jerry has always protected my interests. He has a brother-in-law who's an astute financial adviser, and Jerry put me in touch with him early in my career. Thanks to Ben, my financial future's as secure as anyone's could be. Left to my own devices, I probably would have had to stay with acting until my face muscles started to sag. I'd never had any money. I wouldn't have known how to handle the kind of money I've made on my own."

"Jerry's brother-in-law advised you to buy all those places you own?"

Paul nodded. "They're excellent investments, which is good—because in the long run I don't think I want to keep any of them. Ben would want me to be sure not to sell unless we were dealing in an optimum real-estate market. But rentals do very well, and I've primarily used the chalet in Aspen and the place in Antigua as rental properties. I seldom go to either myself."

"But you ski."

"Yes, I ski. But Aspen isn't the only place in the world where a person can ski."

"And you're a professional quality tennis player."

He laughed. "I still can't believe you've read a lot of the garbage that's been printed about me, sweetheart. I'm a reasonably decent tennis player, yes, but I'm not about to try for the U.S. Open, I assure you. You can take me on anytime you want."

"I ski," Pam admitted, "but I've never played tennis."

"So, I'll teach you."

"What about your condo in Manhattan? You do live there most of the time, don't you?"

"I did. Now... well, what comes next depends..."

"On what you do next?"

"Partly." Paul frowned slightly. "How well do you like Vermont?"

She pulled back, scanned his face. "I love Vermont. Why do you ask?"

"Because not long after I bought the place here at Bryant Lake I began to realize this is where I want to be. A lot of the time, anyway. Not at Bryant Lake all the time. I'd like to buy a sugar bush, Pam."

"A sugar bush?"

"Local name for a grove where you grow maple trees for their syrup."

"I know what a sugar bush is, Mr. Martin."

"That's what I'd like to do," Paul said. "I've been reading up on the subject for the better part of three years. I've driven around and scanned the territory. I'd decided when I came up this year that I'd get in touch with a real-estate agent so I could look over available properties. But, I sort of got sidetracked."

Pam said, "I thought you already had a business in Connecticut . . . or was that just a ruse?"

"No. I do own a controlling interest in a small company near New London that manufactures computer components. But that's an investment—I've no desire to take an active part in running the company. Ben keeps an eye on the operation for me."

Paul fell silent. Then he tugged Pam a little closer and nuzzled her cheek before he said, "You wouldn't even have to change your name, you know."

"What?"

"If you married me. Then we wouldn't have to worry about whether Henry Beeman got our mail mixed up. Yes, I know he's the one who spotted me. Bert told Jerry and Jerry told me. Jerry had to stop by Bert's yesterday after he left your place because he knew he wouldn't be around if Bert phoned to say Angela had arrived on the scene. So Jerry went over to the inn himself and left word for Angela that the two of us would meet her there and . . ."

Paul was talking too fast—and he sounded very unsure of himself.

Pam said quietly, "Paul?"

"Yes?"

"Am I mistaken, or did you propose to me?"

Paul sat up, swung his legs over the side of the bed and kept his back to her as he said in a muffled voice, "I just proposed to you."

"Well, don't you usually look at someone when you've just asked them to marry you?"

"I wouldn't know." Paul's voice was still muffled. "I've never asked anyone to marry me before."

"Tell me one thing."

"What?"

"Jerry left New York fairly early Saturday morning to come back up here."

"So?"

"How did he manage to buy the rings for you before he left the city? I wouldn't think any jewelers would have been open for business that early."

Paul turned around and faced her. A reluctant smile tugged at the corners of his mouth. "Jerry has another brother-in-law, Howard," he said. "Howard happens to own one of the most exclusive jewelry establishments in Manhattan. I told Jerry exactly what I wanted, Howard opened up his store for Jerry and the two of them worked it out."

Paul added, "I can see, though, that those rings might have—well, a bad memory for you. I don't expect you to want them and if you don't we can get something else. If, that is, you're going to consider accepting any ring at all from me..."

His voice trailed off. Pam watched him, and decided that for a man who'd inspired romantic fantasies in at least half the women in the country, he was amazingly humble.

"I don't want another ring, thank you. I'd like my rings back. Just one at a time, though. We ought to save the second one until we've made a few plans. It wouldn't do to leave Jerry out of what we're going to do, would it?"

Paul shook his head slowly then said huskily, "Pam, don't...unless you're very sure."

Pam said softly, "I'm very sure, darling. I'm very, very sure."

Paul still hadn't entirely learned what it was to trust someone. She could see that. But it was a lesson she was prepared to teach him . . . for the rest of their lives.

* * * * *

NORA ROBERTS

Love has a language all its own, and for centuries, flowers have symbolized love's finest expression. Discover the language of flowers—and love—in this romantic collection of 48 favorite books by bestselling author Nora Roberts.

Starting in February 1992, two titles will be available each month at your favorite retail outlet.

In February, look for:

Irish Thoroughbred, Volume #1
The Law Is A Lady, Volume #2

Collect all 48 titles and become fluent in the Language of Love.

LOL192

THE LANGUAGE of LOVE

DONAVAN
Diana Palmer

Diana Palmer's bestselling LONG, TALL TEXANS series continues with DONAVAN....

From the moment elegant Fay York walked into the bar on the wrong side of town, rugged Texan Donavan Langley knew she was trouble. But the lovely young innocent awoke a tenderness in him that he'd never known...and a desire to make her a proposal she couldn't refuse....

Don't miss DONAVAN by Diana Palmer, the ninth book in her LONG, TALL TEXANS series. Coming in January...only from Silhouette Romance.

LTT192

Silhouette Special Edition

salutes

MOMENTS OF GLORY

from Lindsay McKenna

In a country torn with conflict, in a time of bitter passions, these brave men and women wage a war against all odds . . . and a timeless battle for honor, for fleeting moments of glory, for the promise of enduring love.

February: RIDE THE TIGER (#721) Survivor Dany Villard is wise to the love-'em-and-leave-'em ways of war, but wounded hero Gib Ramsey swears she's captured his heart . . . forever.

March: ONE MAN'S WAR (#727) The war raging inside brash and bold Captain Pete Mallory threatens to destroy him, until Tess Ramsey's tender love guides him toward peace.

April: OFF LIMITS (#733) Soft-spoken Marine Jim McKenzie saved Alexandra Vance's life in Vietnam; now he needs her love to save his honor. . . .

SEMG-1

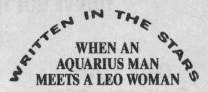
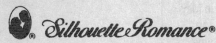